DEAD OR ALIVE!

When Grif saw the gunmen, they were so close that he reached out to squeeze Tom Fry's arm. They were slipping along the boardwalk across the street. If Aimee had run true to form, they would immediately turn their guns upon this alley where they stood like two erect shadows. But they didn't. One of them reached for the door of the Wells Fargo office and tried the knob. He stepped back, and very suddenly the pair stepped together to the door, slammed it open, and poured a flashing barrage of shots into the dummy before the safe.

Tom Fry and Grif stepped into the street and, just as the men stepped back, Grif spoke: "Takin' you boys, dead or alive. Your choice."

Tom's long mule-whip snaked out as one of the pair started on a sprint for the alley that flanked the stage office. The man tripped and went down, but he rolled over and came up to fire one shot. . . .

STAGE TRAILS WEST

FRANK BONHAM

LEISURE BOOKS   NEW YORK CITY

A LEISURE BOOK®

February 2003

Published by special arrangement with Golden West Literary Agency.

Dorchester Publishing Co., Inc.
276 Fifth Avenue
New York, NY 10001

ISBN: 0-8439-5149-4

The name "Leisure Books" and the stylized "L" with design are trademarks of
Dorchester Publishing Co., Inc.

Printed in the United States of America.

Visit us on the web at www.dorchesterpub.com.

Table of Contents

Foreword

by
Bill Pronzini

Frank Bonham (1914–1988) made his first professional sale at the age of 21, of a mystery story to *Phantom Detective*, after which he spent three years learning the craft of fiction writing as a "ghost" for the legendary pulp hack, Ed Earl Repp. Between 1941 and 1951, he contributed millions of words of Western and historical adventure fiction to a variety of pulp magazines, as well as to such slicks as *Liberty* and *Esquire*. His first novel, LOST STAGE VALLEY, appeared from Simon & Schuster in 1948. Over the next forty years he penned eighteen more, among them such stand-outs as NIGHT RAID (Ballantine, 1954), HARDROCK (Ballantine, 1958), CAST A LONG SHADOW (Simon & Schuster, 1964), and THE EYE OF THE HUNTER (M. Evans, 1989). His other credits include three collections of Western stories—THE WILD BREED (Lion, 1955), THE BEST WESTERN STORIES OF FRANK BONHAM (Ohio University Press, 1989), and THE CAÑON OF MAVERICK BRAND: A WESTERN TRIO (Five Star Westerns, 1997)—three mystery novels, twenty-six young adult novels, and scripts for such television shows as "Tales of Wells Fargo" and "Death Valley Days."

While many of his contemporaries specialized in conventional cowboy stories, Bonham utilized a much broader range of Western characters and settings. His protagonists were mountain men, fur traders, freighters, mustangers, miners, doctors, attorneys, gamblers, rodeo performers, and men involved in the vast network of frontier transportation—bold, forward-looking individuals of honor and integrity who stand ready to fight for what they believe is right, even if theirs happens to be an unpopular stand. Seldom does a gunfighter, lawman, or outlaw appear as the central figure of one of his tales. And when he did feature a cowhand or cattleman, it was generally within the framework of an unconventional plot.

Bonham's subject matter and backgrounds are as authentic as meticulous research could make them. Most effective are his tales of the Southwest, in particular Arizona (where he made his home for many years), and those that feature such modes of transportation as riverboats, trains, and stagecoaches. He was particularly adept at recreating the excitement and adventure of stage travel in the latter half of the 19th Century and the conflicts inherent in that rugged, competitive, and often violent industry. In the owners, drivers, shotgun messengers, trouble-shooters, and passengers who people numerous short stories and such novels as LOST STAGE VALLEY and LAST STAGE WEST (Dell, 1959) he created a fascinating array of colorful and eccentric personalities. Perhaps the most memorable of these is Grif Holbrook, his only Western series character.

Hard-bitten, salty, yet kind-hearted, Holbrook is a grizzled veteran of the stage trails who worked as a shotgun guard and trouble-shooter for the Butterfield line for many years prior to the War Between the States. Weary of the life, his dream is to move to California and find "a red-haired widder woman" with whom to settle down; yet, staging is in his blood, and there is nothing he likes more than a challenge. He wears a snakeskin belt with a large silver buckle studded with chip diamonds in the form of a stagecoach, a present from John Butterfield. His weapon of choice is a .44 cap-and-ball "half-breed Colt," fitted with a shoulder stock concealing a whisky canteen in its walnut bosom.

Grif Holbrook made his first appearance in "Hell Along the Oxbow Route" in *Dime Western* (11/44) and reappeared in three short novels published in the same magazine the following year. Bonham chose not to feature him again in a pulp story, but he did make him the protagonist of LOST STAGE VALLEY, which utilizes the same basic premise of "Hell Along the Oxbow Route," but with different secondary characters and plot development. Set in the turbulent period just prior to the outbreak of the War Between the States, "Hell Along the Oxbow Route" deals with the systematic thefts of Butterfield coaches and horses by a gang of Copperheads bent on seizing control of the stage line for the Confederacy. Holbrook is given the job of putting an end to the thefts. His search for the missing coaches and his unmasking of the leader of the gang are pure pulp action fare, lightning-paced and filled with flashing fists and blazing six-guns; but, as in the three subsequent short novels and in Bonham's many novels, the story also contains sharply drawn characters and backgrounds with liberal doses of romance, irony, and personal redemption.

Holbrook has a new employer in "Bullets Blaze the Stage Trails," capitalist Ben Holladay who in 1863 gained control of Butterfield's Great Northern Overland through foreclosure. Sent by Holladay to California's Sierra Nevada to negotiate the purchase of two small independent stage outfits operating between Placerville and Carson City, so as to provide the Union Army with a through stage line to Sacramento without toll stops and toll charges, Holbrook soon finds himself embroiled in a takeover plot by ruthless Bear Flag Rebels.

Among the characters whose path he crosses here are a religious zealot, a wealthy cattle rancher whose home is a castle-like fortress, and the "red-headed widder woman" of his dreams, Annie Benson, owner of one of the jerk-line stage outfits.

Cheyenne, Wyoming Territory, three years later forms the background for "U.P. Trail Breaker." Now at the end of his Great Overland staging days, the result of the imminent completion of the Union Pacific railroad line connecting California to the Union, Holbrook is recruited by General Dodge, Chief of Construction of the U.P., to find out why the company's grade foreman is having difficulty establishing a viable plan for trestling through the Black Hills. A bitter incident in the grade foreman's past, a land-peddling promoter, a rag-tag group of settlers, and a band of Sioux scalp-hunters figure prominently in the story—as does stubborn Annie Benson, now a small cattle rancher whose land is sought by both the U.P. and the unscrupulous promoter. These elements, plus a howling blizzard, a newly built trestle which may or may not be in danger of collapse, and a desperate race against time by rail make "U.P. Trail Breaker" the second best of the Grif Holbrook tales.

Bets of the quartet is "The Buckskin-Popper's War," in which Holbrook returns to staging, this time as a half-interest partner with a woman named Kate Gillison in the short-line Mountain Stage Company in California's Mother Lode. Their attempt to hire stage hands for their new enterprise is complicated by the owner of a rival stage line, the unscrupulous head of the local grange, a shady hydraulic mining company, and a cunning land-grab scheme. The action here is highlighted by a wild stagecoach race and a climactic battle involving monitors and tons of water.

These early stories by Frank Bonham, while not as polished as his later work, are nonetheless good, action-packed entertainment of the sort the Western pulp magazines provided in abundance in the first half of the 20th Century.

Hell Along the Oxbow Route

I

The hotel room was filled with the late afternoon sun and the rich animal odors from the stage yard below. The hostlers were getting a Concord ready, and Grif Holbrook was glad he would be on it, after sitting around El Paso waiting for John Butterfield.

Butterfield sat by the window with a drink, but his flushed countenance was no tribute to his own stages, which had brought him here. He wore a crisp gray beard, and his eyes were wise, as though he had looked on trouble and pleasure and had profited from each.

"Grif," he said, "arguin' with you is like runnin' on a treadmill . . . you always wind up where you started."

Grif Holbrook kept on stuffing socks and shirts into a canvas telescope bag. There was nothing pretty about Grif Holbrook except the way he could shoot a .44 "half-breed" Colt from the deck of a jouncing Concord.

"What do I want with a thousand dollars, anyway?" he argued. "I've already got a thousand. Matter of fact, what do you want with any more money? You've got a steamer line, a freight line, and Lord knows what else. Set down and spend some of that money, John."

Butterfield's broad forehead wrinkled.

"You mean I should let 'em keep on running the Great Southern Overland into the ground because I don't need the money? In the last six months the Oxbow Route has lost eighteen stages and a hundred and eight horses. I've had four drivers killed, both on this all-fired Dragoon run."

"Call in the Army," Grif said. "Me, I'm just an old shotgun messenger headin' for Californy. I got enough money, and I got a big diamond ring in my pocket that I'm going to slip on the finger of the first red-headed widder I meet."

"Sure," Butterfield said. "You take my money all these years, and then you walk out on me when I really need you. Well, there's lots more men that can shoot a gun."

Grif grinned at him. "Don't break down, Johnny," he said. "Who shoved that freight line through the mud and snakes down in Panama? And who cleaned the Indians out that tore down your telegraph line? Me . . . old Grif! And now he wants a rest."

Butterfield asked a question that seemed entirely irrelevant. "How do you stand on the slavery question, Grif?"

Grif said: "What's that got to do with it?" He hitched up his snakeskin belt, with its large silver buckle studded with chip diamonds in the form of a stagecoach. That had been a present from John Butterfield the day the first Oxbow stage rolled into San Francisco. "Why," Grif added, "I guess I'm a Lincoln man, myself. I reckon any man's got a right to work for who he wants. Likewise, he should be able to quit if he wants."

"My sentiments," Butterfield said. "But there's a few million people here that aim to keep their slaves if they have to secede to do it. And you know what'll happen to the Great Southern Overland if war comes!"

Grif said: "I suppose you'll take it North."

The stage man pointed the cigar at him. "You bet I will! And everybody in the South knows it." He threw the cigar angrily out the window, while his gray eyes hardened. "Someone's out to wreck the greatest stage line in the world, so that, by the time war comes, it'll either have gone into Southern hands, or there'll be nothing left! Right now the Dragoon link is about to snap. Pretty soon no driver will tackle it and passengers won't attempt it. When that happens, the game's over. California looks secessionist. She'll pull the Western half out of my reach, and the South will do the same for the Eastern. Whereas, if I can hold it intact until the moment to git, it will mean more to the North than ten thousand troops."

Grif Holbrook had been a long time with John Butterfield. They had pulled their way through some lean times together; the Great Southern was only the final glorious result of a monument they had been many years chipping at.

Grif was no kid; he had a ranch picked out to buy in California, where he could make money without risking his life every day. A month ago Butterfield had written to him, saying that he wanted to have a farewell drink with him before he quit. A sly one, John Butterfield, because the farewell drink was just a come-on to the toughest job he had thrown at him yet.

Grif said in an upsurge of stubbornness: "I . . . I can't do it. I risked my life too damn' often, John. I got a future to think of."

John Butterfield said: "I'm sorry for you. When the North has lost, they'll be sounding taps over a lot of young fellas that were too young to die. And what the bugle will be sayin' is . . . 'They died in vain, because Grif Holbrook was afraid to risk a few scratches on his hide!' " The king of the stage trails rose, offered Grif his hand, smiling bitterly: "But that's up to you, Grif. I wish you luck."

Grif threw a last sock at the valise. "Oh, hell," he said. "Why didn't you say that in the first place and save us all this rag-chewin'?"

Butterfield smiled, took a deep breath. His whole vast do-main rested on the shoulders of a few trusted men, and of them all he had chosen Grif to thrust his finger in the leaking dike.

Butterfield saw Grif unsling the Dragoon Colt that he carried under his shoulder. It was a .44 cap-and-ball, fitted with a shoulder stock, which in turn was eccentric by virtue of concealing a canteen in its walnut bosom. Grif took a long pull at it, then he blew out his cheeks. He carried dynamite at both ends of his gun.

"The details are up to you," Butterfield told him. "There's a thousand for you when you finish the job, an expense account for all you need. You can get the lowdown from Senator Blaise Montgomery, in Dragoon. He's acting as agent for me. An Alabaman, but loyal as can be. Served three terms in the Senate until he opened his mouth in the wrong argument. Now he's in Arizona Territory for his health."

Outside, the note of the stage horn went sharply through the dusty heat. Grif slung the revolver under his black coat, closed his valise, pulled the greasy lanyard of his Stetson up under his chin, and grudgingly put out his hand. "Well, so long," he said. "If they knock me over, write me an epitaph like this . . . 'Here lies Grif Holbrook. You could talk him into anything.' "

II

The Concord rolled up the valley road, in and out of motes of yellow and salt cedar. Beside the road the Río Grande was a shallow ribbon of brown water dotted with sandbars. Mexican farmers had their corn and chile patches in the rich bottomlands, neat and green, but the slopes that mounted to the abrupt base of the Franklins were a dry, barren world of ocotillo and greasewood.

A girl in a brown alpaca traveling cape and a demure poke bonnet sat between Grif and a stout man who had the look of a drummer. Across from them was an elderly, prosperous-appearing man, between whom and a younger, ruggedly handsome man at the other window was sandwiched another woman—young, Grif saw, and somehow familiar to him.

Familiar! She was the little redhead he'd had aboard when a bunch of Comanches had jumped them down Van Horn way last March! Grif saw that she was regarding him with the same interest. He began to flick specks of dust from his coat, wishing he had shaved that morning.

She leaned forward, smiling. "Why, *you're* Mister Holbrook!" she said. "I'm Aimee Prentiss. Remember?"

Grif grinned. "I see that little scrape with our feathered friends didn't sour you on the Butterfield line."

Aimee shook her red curls. She was nicely stacked up, he thought, and possessed of violet eyes that were downright wicked, accented by the ridges of high cheek bones.

"Of course it didn't," she said. "You were wonderful, Mister Holbrook. How is it you aren't on the box this time?"

Grif hesitated, heeding the whispering of caution. "I've retired. Headin' for Californy to buy a ranch."

"How romantic!" Aimee Prentiss turned to the man beside her. "Why can't *we* do something like that, Bud, instead of traveling around selling saloon fixtures?"

Her husband gave Grif a sour look. "Because I don't know port from starboard on a cow."

Grif's ambition was dampened by the knowledge that Aimee Prentiss was married. *Hell,* he told himself, *I'm too old for such foolishness anyhow*. But Aimee said: "How many outlaws have you killed, Mister Holbrook?"

Grif flushed. "I never figgered it up," he said.

Bud Prentiss snorted and hunched down in his seat. "I feel real safe, having you along, Holbrook," he said. "You must be awful brave."

Aimee sniffed. "You're just jealous, Bud."

Out in the rush of wind and darkness the driver's whip popped faintly. Grif Holbrook, used to these things, got ready for the lunge that was coming. The stage swung into a dry wash, lamps blinking, and with a lurch it went across the sandy groove of a streambed. The stage sagged back on its bull-hide thorough braces; in the next instant it surged forward, with that impetus the horses needed to continue their smooth run. This impetus also served to bring everyone up onto his feet, bang his head into that of the person across from him, and sit him down with a jolt, and, when the confusion ended, Grif Holbrook found a warm, fragrant little bundle on his lap that was Aimee Prentiss.

Aimee giggled. "Oh, Mister Holbrook! I'm so sorry!"

Her husband's voice went through the thick silence with an angry snap. "Get back here, you cheap little . . . !" His hand reached out, and he pulled the girl back to the seat. He said to Grif: "There's a lot of room outside, mister. Maybe you two would like to be alone."

One thing was certain in Grif's mind: he did not care for Bud Prentiss. "Such things will happen, son," he said.

Prentiss, glowering, produced a half-pint bottle from his coat and took a long pull at it.

The valley road was long, with few turns. Now and then they stopped at a swing station and switched teams. Then again they rolled at a steady beat. Fatigue and monotony came to roost in the dark coach, until, at midnight, the Concord swept into the big chinaberry-and-adobe settlement of Mesilla, once capital of all New Mexico Territory. Between

18

solid blocks of dark adobe houses they rolled, the street dust deadening the clatter of two dozen hoofs, the trees shaking their dry leaves as they rushed past.

Through the quiet village went the commanding note of the stage horn, as they approached a long building afire with lamp-yellowed windows. The horses swung into the yard of La Posta with a nicety of skilled reining. The conductor and guard swung open the doors.

"Hour's stop, folks," the conductor said. "Grab some coffee and grub while you can."

The ladies stepped down and went together toward the door. Grif was on the step when he saw Bud Prentiss below him. Prentiss came in swiftly, and he swung a looping blow that caught Grif high on the cheek and plunged him back onto the floor of the stage.

The conductor was swearing. "Here, now! What the tarnation . . . !"

"Leave him be," Grif said, getting out of the coach. "This is the last warnin' you get, feller," he said. "I want an apology."

"Apology!" Prentiss snorted. He closed quickly, his left hand stabbing at Holbrook's face, right hand cocked.

Grif took the first blow on the shoulder. The second did not land, for he had waded inside the man's guard and slugged him on the jaw.

Prentiss scrambled up and came in stubbornly. He lashed at Grif's face, and the stage man sent a stiff left hand against Prentiss's jaw. Then, suddenly, Prentiss was on his knees, and there was something in his hand that caused the stage man to dive with a yell behind the coach.

Grif turned, the Colt flashing up from beneath the skirts of his coat, swinging on its shoulder strap. He saw Bud Prentiss, standing with his left arm hanging and his right extended straight out, pointing the gun as he would have pointed a finger. Then an explosion of flame obscured the picture, and he heard the bullet smash the panel beside his left shoulder. The flame and smoke were gone. Then he was looking at Prentiss across his own gun barrel.

Grif thought: *Miss his arm and you're a dead pigeon! He asked for it.* . . . But when he fired, it was at Prentiss's arm. He wouldn't miss; he played on a Colt as some men played on a fiddle.

Prentiss was down on his knees, groaning, holding his wrist. Grif went over and kicked the gun out of his way. "Some fellers just have to stick their fingers in a buzz saw to see if it's turnin'," he said. "Who paid you to do this, son?"

"Nobody," Prentiss snarled. "I see red every time Aimee starts shinin' up to a man that way."

"You're a liar," Grif said quietly.

Prentiss stood up, biting his lip. "All right," he said. "All I want is a sawbones."

Grif turned to the driver. "Find him a doctor, will you?" he said. "And see to it he don't get back on this stage."

Pushing through the crowd on the hotel porch, Grif was arrested by a large red-faced man who took his arm.

"Suh," he said, "if you are anyone but Mistuh Grif Holbrook, I'll let the bartender crush the mint in my julep!"

Grif saw an elderly man with a shining bald head, in a gray box coat, a black string tie.

"You've got the advantage o' me," Grif said.

The stranger offered a meaty hand. "Senator Blaise Montgomery, suh. Hoped to catch you here and finish the trip in your company. Had to come down yesterday on business."

The senator guided him through the hotel across the street to a saloon. It was a low-grade Mexican *cantina*, but the man moved through the room as though it were the drawing room of his Birmingham mansion.

"After what I have just witnessed," the senator said, "I judge you understand what you have got into. That man Prentiss is almost certainly a spy. We are fightin' as bloodthirsty a pack of rascals as this country has evah seen. I presume John Butterfield mentioned me to you?"

Grif tasted the whisky. "Said you could give me the lowdown. What brought you to Mesilla?"

Senator Montgomery glanced about them. "Guns," he said. "Contraband guns. Word came to me of a shipment of muskets passing through this town. But there was no sign of them by the time I reached here. Gave me the slip, the devils!"

The news put a chill on Grif's flesh. "You talk like we're already at war," he said.

The senator pulled his tangled brows down, slowly wagging his head. "The dogs of war, suh, are as good as unleashed. Soon the blood-tides will lap the very hearth-stones of the humblest home of this proud land. Brothah will take up the saber against brothah, father against son. And it is my own beloved Southland which will suffer the most." He sighed, swishing the liquor about in his glass. "While I was in Washington, I did what I could do to bring reason to the madhouse. Exile was my reward. Now, suh, I'm in danger of my life!"

They went back to the hotel. "Got an idea of who's running this outfit?" Grif asked him.

Montgomery shook his head. "I've had them trailed. The tracks always peter out in the sand flats. Eighty percent of the hold-ups have taken place in Apache Pass. All they want is the coaches and stock."

The senator secured his bag from his room, and Grif saw to stowing it in the boot. When the stagecoach lurched on up the valley and cut due west through rising, dune-barricaded country toward the Mimbres, Senator Montgomery took Prentiss's place. In a corner of the coach, weeping silently, sat Aimee Prentiss—and, whatever she might be, coquette or killer's accomplice, Grif Holbrook's heart wept with her.

III

Through the night they rattled along the rutted stage trail, inching slowly toward the mountains to the northwest. In various attitudes of medieval torture, all the passengers except Grif and the girl in the poke bonnet found sleep.

He saw the small pale oval of her face turn toward him. "I don't suppose you know of a good piano tuner in Dragoon, Mister Holbrook?"

Grif started. "If it was something easy," he said, "like a troupe of Swiss bell-ringers, maybe I could help you. But a piano tuner is something Dragoon hasn't been graced with to date, being that there's only one piano . . . and that's in the Blood Bucket."

The girl looked, Grif thought, right on the verge of tears. "I . . . I didn't realize it would be so primitive. You see, I used to support myself by music lessons in Tennessee. I thought, well . . . there must be children. . . ."

"Got relatives out here, Miss . . . ?"

" . . . Mary Storm," the girl said. "I have a . . . well, he was once a close friend. He's station tender at Apache Pass . . . Tom Fry."

Grif patted her hand. "What happened between him and you, Mary?"

Mary Storm put a wide, frightened glance on him. "He . . . he *killed* a man!" Then she added quickly: "Oh, I don't mean murder! Tom was deputy sheriff in Tiptonville. He *had* to shoot a man in a bank hold-up. But something happened afterward . . . I don't know what . . . and he became very strange. Finally he left. He didn't write for a year. Then he only wrote to say that he wouldn't be back. That'd he'd never wear a sheriff's star again. But I thought . . . I thought if I could only talk to him. . . ."

Grif said slowly: "I wish you luck, miss. But if he's got the disease I think he has, you won't cure him. Gunfighter's fever, they call it."

In the morning they changed drivers and stagecoaches at Cook's Springs, a wind-harried little station at the base of the mountains. They ran on, skirting the hills, while the sun grew hotter and dust swirled and eddied inside the coach. They lunched at a dismal relay called Soldier's Farewell. In the middle of the afternoon they broke through a rampart of flinty hills onto the broad San Simon Valley.

Ahead of them now were the precipitous Chiricahua Mountains and Apache Pass, which coursed a bloody two miles through the range. Grif sat up straighter, leaning out the window to get a clear view ahead. It looked peaceful enough, even pretty, the desert a soft pink and the mountains purple, but, as they rolled along, Grif loaded the extra cylinder of his gun.

At eight o'clock they pulled into the yard of the Apache Pass station, under the frowning battlements of the mountains. The coach lamps played briefly across a long, low building under friendly cottonwoods. A big wooden water tank bulked darkly beyond the house.

They saw Tom Fry, holding a rifle, and several Mexican stock-tenders standing before the shuttered station. Parker, the driver, called down sharply: "What do you think this is,

Fry . . . a sight-seein' excursion? Where's the hosses? I'm behind schedule right now."

Fry, his denim pants cuffed above the spur marks on his boots, said: "This is as far as you're going tonight. Carrying any passengers?"

Parker said: "Six. What do you mean, I'm not going through?"

"Come inside," Tom Fry said. And he walked over and opened the stagecoach door.

He helped Aimee Prentiss out, but Grif kept his seat and watched as Mary Storm put out her hand for Fry to help her down. Fry stared in sudden astonishment. "Mary!"

"I'm just passing through, Tom. And aren't you going to say you're glad to see me?"

"You . . . here!" he said. "You . . . you followed me?"

"Not exactly," she said. "I'm going to stay in Dragoon for a while. I thought I might see you while I was here."

Fry seemed unable to find words. He turned and went to the house to let in the others. Grif followed them into the main room with its bare mud walls and low ceiling.

Somewhere a man cried out, as if in his sleep. Tom Fry turned from bolting the door. "That's why you're not going on," he said. "They jumped the east-bound last night. No passengers aboard, but they killed the driver and guard and wounded the conductor. That's him in the bedroom."

"How did he get here?" the senator asked.

"Crawled, on his hands and knees. He gave me a yarn about a mud wagon appearing from nowhere and crowding them off the road. He said there were ghost horses pulling it, and he swears the driver was Jimmie Judd. I guess he was already out of his head."

The stage men nodded. Jimmie Judd, the big, blond Texan who had been the best whip who ever tooled a rig

24

through the Apache country, had been shot from the box six months ago and ground to a pulp under the wheeler's hoofs. They had buried him on a knoll near the Dragoon road and named a dry wash Judd Creek in his honor.

After the horses were taken care of, the driver, Parker, and the guard and the conductor spread their blankets. Fry and Grif shared the hard dirt floor of the room next to the dying man's. The other men drew the floor of the front room.

While the others ate jack rabbit stew and *frijoles refritos* at the table, Grif watched Tom Fry and Mary. By their expressions Grif knew that all was not well. Fry was a dark-skinned, capable-appearing youngster, but he had brooding eyes and a stubborn mouth, and whatever pebbles of entreaty Mary threw against him bounced off without effect. Finally the girl got up and went to her room.

About nine o'clock everyone went to bed. Grif took off his boots and stretched out on his blankets, thinking about Jimmie Judd and the ghost Concord, about the dangerous run ahead, and he thought about John Butterfield's notion that they were racing against time, that a powerful hand was squeezing his great stage trail in two, right here at Apache Pass. . . . He heard the station-tender sigh.

"I been through it too, son," Grif said. "It's no fun."

"Through what?" Tom Fry asked.

"Sharin' my bed and board with a ghost," the former shot-gun guard told him. "It was three years before I pried the first man I killed out of my brain. Every time I sat down to eat he was sittin' across from me, showin' me the hole in his chest. When I went to bed, he laid beside me, whisperin' . . . 'I was young and full of life myself, once, but you cut me down like a man'd cut a willow switch. Only God has the right to do that.' "

Fry spoke with the heat of desperation. "He was right!

God must punish killers by plaguing them this way!"

"Killers?" Grif said. "I wasn't no killer. I gather you weren't, either. When we bucked those boys, it was us or them, and we were fighting for men not strong enough to fight for themselves. It took me three years to find that out."

Fry said doggedly: "But if I have to brace a man again, I hope to hell he shoots first. It's the one I killed that gets the break."

Grif felt his heart take the reins. *This kid's in trouble,* he thought. *It won't cost me anything to help him.* "Too bad you feel this way," he said. "I could use a man like you. I'm workin' alone in a game where everybody else is a house man." He told Fry what he wanted him to know about the set-up.

Fry grunted. "Funny you should ask help of me," he said. "Or have I lost my Tennessee accent? As a matter of fact, I'm a secessionist myself."

"I reckoned you were," Grif told him. "But in this fight abolitionists and secessionists have got to work shoulder to shoulder. We're not fightin' the battle of North and South. We're fighting over whether any man has the right to kill other men in cold blood, whatever his political party. Did they ask that gent in the next room how he was votin'? And what about Jimmie Judd . . . he was a Texan, and a secessionist the last time I talked to him."

Fry was silent a moment. "That's right," he said slowly. "You mean that this renegade pack is doing the South more harm than good . . . is that it?"

"Son, you named it! Then you'll help out, won't you?"

Fry said: "No! I swore two years ago that I was done with killin' for hire. Good night."

IV

In the morning, Grif helped the stage men hitch up the team. He did not see Tom Fry and Mary Storm say good bye, but when the stage clattered out of the station, there were two forlorn women in it instead of one. The Concord swept up the desolate road that bent and twisted in the pink dawn between steep cliffs.

Parker, the hook-nosed driver, drove with earnest concentration. He had his team loosely strapped and chained so that they ran easily with their heads high. Grif and the conductor were on the deck behind him. The shotgun messenger, with the Wells Fargo box under his seat, was at Parker's side.

A few twisted cedars and black oaks grew along the road. Grif was acutely conscious of the cañon walls, pressing in upon them, of being boxed up like an ox in a slaughter stall. Two miles . . . the bloodiest two miles in Arizona.

His eyes were never still, searching both sides of the road and trying to see around the sharp turns. Thus it struck him like a thunder clap to realize suddenly that a team of horses was drawing in beside them, that almost abreast of them was rocking another stagecoach. He yelled and reared up to pull a bead on the driver. Yet his hands moved as though they were asleep. He tried to squeeze the trigger, and his finger froze. *What's the matter with you?* His mind was yelling that, trying to shake him into action. But Grif Holbrook knew what was the matter. It was that face under his sights.

It was Jimmie Judd—his friend, long dead and buried! Yes, Jimmie was dead, a victim of this same crew of trail pirates that was closing with them right now. And yet it was Texas Jimmie himself who sat alone upon the box of the low-slung mud wagon, nodding pleasantly at them and smiling.

Grif was cold, and he was soaked with perspiration. It was

all like a nightmare—the hearse-like coach with curtains drawn, the horses tossing their heads like wild things, and a ghost holding the ribbons.

He heard a gun roar, but it wasn't his. The flash came from a window of the coach below them. He fired twice at the leather curtain through which the shot had come. He heard two ringing sounds like anvil strokes, and right then he knew what they were up against. They weren't leather curtains. They were boiler-plate. The ghost-wagon was armored.

Then it was Jimmie Judd or nothing. He brought the gun up again. The Concord pulled ahead of them and was beginning to crowd the stage off the road. The women were screaming, and the drummer and his companions had begun to yell and fire haphazardly.

Jimmie Judd sent his long whip out and pulled on the reins, and Parker had to swerve his own team to avoid a tangle. They were crashing along through brush and rocks, the passengers thumping about inside. When the Concord heaved up on two wheels and began to roll over, Grif knew they were done.

He was not consciously frightened. He was looking for a soft spot, and he was feeling bitterness and remorse. This was what John Butterfield had picked him for, and he had failed. He landed a-sprawl, rolling over and over, and he was not quite conscious of when he stopped rolling.

When he opened his eyes, there were men sitting around on the rocks and a huddle of badly shaken passengers under a black oak nearby. He saw five men, two of them masked, pulling the overturned coach upright. Somewhere the senator was loudly declaiming about decency and fair play. Jimmie Judd walked over to Grif. He had Grif's gun under his arm.

"Sorry, pardner," he said. "Just one of those hazards of a hard trade."

Grif looked at the stage driver. "How about a drink?" he said. "There's a canteen in the stock of my gun."

Judd inspected the Dragoon gun, grinning. "Quite a contraption. But I don't know as it would be very good sense to arm you, Grif. You're *mucho hombre* with a smoke-pole."

Grif waved his hand. "The cylinder comes out. You've got my powder and shot flask. What you worrying about?"

Judd opened the canteen, tilted the gun stock, and drank generously. Afterwards, he gave it to Grif.

In addition to the two masked men helping with the stage, there were two other outlaws on the deck of the armored Concord, keeping the passengers under their sights. One of the men came from the coach as it rocked back onto four wheels and the team was backed into the traces. He spoke to Jimmie Judd. "All set," he said. It was a pleasant, deep-South voice, and they were pleasant gray eyes behind holes in the mask. He carried a heavy sporting rifle with a revolving cylinder; the fingers that held it were slender and tapered.

Grif caught the gray eyes while he asked: "Are you going to harm the women?"

The other man chuckled. "I'm afraid our reputation has gotten out of hand," he said. "John Butterfield is our enemy, not his helpless passengers. As a matter of fact, sir, the stage will go on directly."

"Then," Grif shrugged, "what have you accomplished?"

Judd grinned. "We've got you, Grif. That's what we've accomplished."

Parker climbed back up on the box with his guard. The drummer and the other passenger got back in after the women. Senator Montgomery made a last appeal. "Gentlemen," he said, "there's such a thing as Constitutional rights. . . ."

One of the outlaws snapped—"Save it for the Senate,

pop."—and he slammed the door and shouted: "Roll 'em!" Parker gave Grif a hopeless glance. Then the stagecoach rolled around the bend.

Jimmie Judd did not waste time. He sprang to the driver's seat, while the other four men loaded Grif into the coach. Grif had an unpleasant sensation of passing through a door into a dark world, beyond anything he knew. Windowless, the cab required a lamp at each side to break the darkness. The outlaws sat in their white hoods with their guns across their knees. It was like riding in a hearse with four ghosts for company.

He noticed that the right sleeve of one of the men was empty. This man carried only a revolver. Suddenly it was as though a rag had been passed over a dusty window, letting light through.

"How's the arm, Prentiss?" Grif asked.

The man with the Colt started, but did not answer. Grif went on, smiling. "I couldn't help wonderin' how my old pard Jimmie knew I was coming. I suppose you and Aimee were spying on me and Butterfield in El Paso, and you come ahead to give the word."

The man chuckled.

"Tell me something," Grif said. He began to grope in his pockets. "I could use a smoke, fellers." Someone tossed him a sack of tobacco, and he began to roll a smoke. "What I'd like to know," Grif went on, "is how Jimmie Judd can be up there on the box, and be buried beside Judd's Creek all at once."

The man with the gray eyes said softly: "I could arrange the same for you."

"What do you mean?"

Bud Prentiss's voice came through the mask. "We'll tell you what we want you to know, Holbrook. If I had my way. . . ."

"If you had your way," interrupted the gray-eyed man, "we'd have had so many killings the Army would have been called in by now."

For a moment there was silence, the stagecoach rattling and banging as it tipped sharply upward.

The man spoke again. "Grif, I'm looking for a running mate for Jimmie. He needs more protection up there on the box. I'm giving you a choice . . . you can join us or find a grave out here."

Grif said: "I think I know what you're fightin' for, pardner, but I don't like the way you're goin' about it. You're giving your cause a black eye with the whole country."

The Southerner said quietly: "Suppose we are. We're helping the South, and we're helping ourselves. Eventually the entire Great Southern will be under our control. Then we'll dictate terms to certain interests who know the virtue of such a road. You can share in the take when it comes through."

The man's eyes were on every move Grif made. Four guns were on him, and all he could say was: "It's hell to have a conscience. It keeps you from ever having any fun, and sometimes it puts a rope around your neck. I can't do it. The answer is no."

He leaned forward, half rising, to hold his newly built cigarette above the chimney of the lamp and puff it to life. He saw the revolver in Prentiss's hand rise. Then he made his play.

V

His breath went sharply across the lamp chimney, and, as it puffed out, he tore the hot chimney loose and slammed it against the other lamp across the coach. In the sudden blackness

31

men were shouting, but no one dared shoot for fear of hitting a comrade. In his hand Grif had one of the spare cylinders that he had reloaded in the pass. He crammed it into his gun.

The gray-eyed man's voice came: "Don't lose your heads, gentlemen. Sit perfectly still. If you feel anyone moving near you, place your gun against him and shoot."

Grif Holbrook was plowing across the floor, trampling toes and arches, then crashing against the door. The catch gave, and Grif was blinded by the sudden burst of sunlight. He had a dazzling picture of a steep mountain road and abrupt hillsides lightly timbered with stunted desert trees. His immediate concern was the rough ground slipping beneath him as he sailed into the brush. He heard the flat bark of a gun, and then, for the second time in an hour, he piled headlong against the earth.

His left arm went dead, while the pain from a wrenched shoulder socket twisted through him. But he was conscious when he came to rest on the reddish earth. That was all he asked for.

The stage had stopped a couple hundred feet beyond. Jimmie Judd was looking back, startled. He reached for his carbine, and Grif aimed his gun and fired.

Judd hunched over, letting the rifle drop, and disappeared from sight behind the decking. Grif swung the gun down to cover the open door of the Concord. A man sprang through, running for a rock. Grif knocked him over like a jack rabbit. Another man started through, saw what had happened, and ducked back. Grif threw a ball against the iron door of the stagecoach, and the shot glanced inside, bringing a yell.

Grif heard the gray-eyed Southerner shouting: "Jimmie! Get this thing rolling! He's got us in a pocket!"

He saw Jimmie Judd drag himself up on the seat. He got Judd's head on his front sight. But he couldn't shoot.

The stage rolled, the door banging shut. Grif went up, his shoulder so sore he could hardly bear to move his arm. A fifteen-minute climb put him on a wind-combed ridge from which he could see, to the west, the flat brown table of the desert. Very faintly he could make out the straight thread of the stage trail pointing toward Dragoon. The ghost wagon had disappeared to the north. He could see it, now and then, but he knew it would not stay long on such a plainly marked road.

Grif had trudged only a mile or two when he heard hoofs behind him and the bumbling echoes of a wagon. He spotted a steeple-like rock, and he was sprawled at its base when a string of mules filed past the nearest bend. A high-sided freight wagon lumbered into view, and behind it another hitched to the first, and following the last a small water wagon. The mule-skinner on the seat had one leg cocked over the side, and the cotton jerk-line was wrapped lightly about his ankle. He sent out across the team's head a long whip.

Grif watched him all the way from the turn until he was abreast of the rock. Particularly he wanted to know if the big freight wagons had gun loops in their high sides. But he found nothing suspicious, either in the wagons or in the big blond mule-skinner on the seat. At the proper moment he stepped out and lifted his hand.

The freighter, a man of ponderous muscles and knuckle-scarred features, pulled in his team. "Are you some kind of a rare shrub, mister," he said, "or do I jest *think* I see you?"

"You see me, all right," Grif said. "I had a little altercation with some road agents. If you got room for another up there, I'd shore like to save some boot leather."

The mule-skinner spat, studying Grif. "Climb up," he offered. "Name of Sig Johnson," he said. "I'm up from El Paso by way of Skeleton Cañon and the Cherrycows. Not many bullwhackers have got the craw for the El Paso-Dragoon run these days. Lucky I run across you."

"Plenty," Grif said. He told him about his brush with the renegade gang. Sig Johnson was full of interest.

"It's strange doin's," he said. "They don't bother nothing much but the coach and hosses. Lord knows what they do with 'em. They claim there's a spot called Stagecoach Valley somewheres in these mountains where every coach and hoss Butterfield's lost is penned up. But the story has it that there's only one trail into Stagecoach Valley, and it goes through a gorge where one man could hold off a regiment."

Night overtook them on the desert, still fifteen miles from Dragoon. They slept under the wagons and were up again before dawn. About noon they dragged into the ugly, sun-baked town of Dragoon.

There was a hotel, one-storied and with small, thick-silled windows. Across from it was the Blood Bucket Saloon. Spotted here and there among other dismal dwellings were the stage office, a barbershop, a blacksmith shop. Senator Montgomery must have been pretty sick to have come to Dragoon, Grif thought.

Sig Johnson pulled in his team before the Blood Bucket. A few men drifted out to see the newcomers, and Johnson jumped quickly down.

"Will Moriarty's got a couple of spare rooms behind the saloon," he said. "Hotel'll rob you blind. Moriarty'll be out directly."

Grif said—"Thanks."—and started up the street. A small-ish man in a brown suit came from the saloon. His hair and long sideburns were almost white, but the face was that of a man in his late thirties.

Johnson greeted him heartily—"Howdy, Will!"—and the saloon owner made a salute with a lax hand.

"How many bottles did you forget to break?" he asked Johnson.

Johnson cut at his boots with his whip. "Never broke a bottle yet, you old chuckwalla!"

Inside the barbershop, it was stiflingly hot, Grif found; flies buzzed in and out, and the snores of the barber were loud in the heavy silence. Grif whistled once, and the bald, red-faced man started up in the chair. "What'll it be, friend?" he said.

"A bath," Grif said. "And then the works."

The barber opened a booth in the back and glanced outside. "Yep," he said. "Last gent left the towel as clean as he found it. There's bull-tallow soap if you're the greasy kind, store-bought if you ain't. I'll bring fresh water. They call me Bay-Rum Brown, friend. Glad to form your acquaintance."

When he smelled the barber's breath, Grif understood where he got his name. He was sitting in the wooden barrel, dipping water over himself with a gourd, when he heard spurred boots come into the shop. There was more than one man; maybe two, he thought. When he heard the first man's voice, it was as though the water he was pouring over his head had been suddenly chilled.

"We're in a hurry, Bay-Rum," the stranger said. "Just a quick once-over today."

The voice was the quiet, deep-South voice of the man with the gray eyes.

VI

Grif learned two things: the man's name was Johnny Burns; his companion was referred to as Salty. Bay-Rum's dexterous razor went over the jowls of them both in ten minutes. Grif dressed.

Then the man called Johnny said: "Doc Benteen around to-day?"

"You didn't miss him a half hour!" Bay-Rum said. "He's just rode up to Dud Paxsen's. Dud's down with mountain fever."

"A friend of mine is pretty sick down at the saloon," Johnny Burns said. "We'll go after him."

Grif walked out of the cubicle. He wanted to see if Johnny Burns's nerves were as good as his. Grif stood at the mirror, adjusting his tie. Salty was in the chair being talcumed, a knotty little customer with pale eyes and red sideburns. Johnny Burns was waiting by the door. He was young, in his middle twenties, his eyes gray as a December sky.

Grif nodded. "Howdy. You the man's looking for a doc?"

Burns smiled. "Why, yes."

"I've done a little pill-rollin'," Grif said. "Maybe I could help."

"Afraid not," Burns said. "This is a broken bone."

Grif said: "Oh."

After Salty got out of the chair, Grif took it, spreading a month-old St. Louis newspaper across his knees. He did not look up when they left. When Bay-Rum Brown saw Grif's half-breed Colt, he grunted. "Say," he said, "you wouldn't be Grif Holbrook, would you?"

"I might," Grif told him.

"Feller name of Tom Fry was looking for you today," the barber said. "He mentioned that gun. He's stayin' at the Desert Rest. Understand he's quit his job at Apache Pass. The senator sent a replacement out this afternoon. They don't last long, by golly!"

Grif Holbrook went out into the dry heat of the sun-blazed street, feeling the sweat pop out on his jowls. The encounter with Johnny Burns had pleased him. He had avoided gun play

36

because he wanted Burns to lead him to the kingpin of the stage-pirate ring. In the interim he might look up Tom Fry.

Fry had a room at the corner of the hotel, on the shady side. When Grif entered, Fry did not get up; he lay on the bed with his fingers linked under his head. "This isn't for you or John Butterfield, see?" he said. "It's for the South. I got to thinking about it, and it looks like it's time for action. But I'll be damned if I'll carry a gun."

"Damned if you do, and killed if you don't," Grif said. "But I'm glad to have you, anyway. Seen Mary?"

Fry looked both angry and puzzled. "She's working for the senator. Secretary. I offered to help her, but she wouldn't take anything."

"You didn't figger she would, did you?" Grif said. "That girl's got pride. *And* courage."

In Fry's eyes Grif saw confusion and despair, and maybe a little shame.

"I may be needing you tonight, or sooner," Grif told him. "Stick around where I can find you."

In the Blood Bucket, a pasty-faced man at the piano was playing an accompaniment for a girl who sat on the top of the battered instrument, singing in a tinselly voice. She was wearing a close-fitting gown with spangles and frou-frou, and the way it demonstrated the female figure took Grif's breath. It took his breath still more when he realized it was Aimee Prentiss.

Will Riordan, the saloonkeeper, sat with a barman at a round table. He was waving his cigar in time to the music. The tune ended.

"You'll do, Aimee," Riordan said. "Sing that one about 'Mother' again. The boys will like that."

The professor rolled out a two-foot arpeggio, and Grif

took a chair beside Riordan. Aimee Prentiss jumped from the piano and came quickly to the table. Riordan gave Grif a hard, quick glance. "What do you want, mister?" he asked.

"I'm a friend of Sig Johnson's," Grif said. "Sig said you had a couple of rooms."

"Both taken."

Grif looked up at the redhead. "How's Bud?"

Aimee shook her head. "I don't know, Mister Holbrook. I . . . I wanted to say that I'm sorry about what happened. Bud's a crazy-jealous fool."

"He's a busy fool, too," Grif told her. "He was on the Concord that shanghaied me."

Aimee said: "No!"

"Yep. I guess you know it means hanging if I catch him. Same for the rest of them."

The girl bit her lip. "I know," she said. "He got in with that crowd in El Paso. I begged him not to fool with them. Now . . . he's got to face it."

Grif looked at her, not unconscious of the way tears enhanced her deep-blue eyes. *A red-headed widder,* he thought. He said softly: "It's too bad, Aimee. . . . I'll just cut through the back way and see how Sig's makin' out."

As he went past a door in the rear, he could hear a moan. Sig Johnson and a couple of swampers were unloading long, flat boxes from the wagons. A few kegs were ranged beside the door, and there were cases of hard liquor stacked in the shade. Grif Holbrook studied the long boxes, trying to puzzle out what a saloonkeeper would buy that came in a container of that description. He stood there until he heard the clatter of the piano. Then he went back into the saloon and opened the door of the sick man's room.

Jimmie Judd was lying on a cot, propped up against the wall with a gun across his knees. He was flushed, and his eyes were as bright as glass beads. He jerked the gun up when he saw Grif.

"No, you lousy sawbones!" he croaked. "I'll shoot your damned guts out before you take off my leg!"

"Nobody's going to cut your leg off, Jimmie," Grif said softly. "It's Grif. Just wanted to talk."

Judd seemed confused. "Grif?"

Grif pulled up a chair. "I'm sorry, Jimmie," he said. "You should have stuck to stagin'."

Judd let his head lie back against the wall, and Grif knew that it would either be death or amputation of that infected leg. It was not pleasant to reflect that he had put the ball into him that had brought him to this.

"I reckon you're right," Jimmie Judd said, and he tried to grin. "I know I done wrong, but that don't make this tarnal leg feel any better."

"Would it make it feel better, maybe," Grif asked him, "to clear your conscience? I got a job ahead of me. It would help a lot if I could just pick off the big boys. I don't care about the others . . . dime-a-dozen gunslingers. What they don't know, and what you didn't know, is that this shebang is being run for one or two men's profit. Johnny Burns, for one, another I don't know yet. Do you?"

Jimmie Judd looked at him. "How do you know it's a two-man game?"

"I got a head, Jimmie. I know this isn't helping the South's chances any. Burns himself told me the idea was to sell it out after he had control. Maybe a damn' Yankee . . . I don't know. But don't try to tell me it will be a ten- or twenty-way split."

The Texan writhed under a sudden twist of pain. When he came out of it, he was sweating. "By God, if I thought that was true . . . !" he gasped. "I don't care about the money. But when war comes, the South will need the Oxbow."

"So will the North," Grif said. "Who's the big boy, Jimmie?"

He thought the name was on the stage man's lips, but just then the door opened and Bud Prentiss was in the portal. Prentiss had a Colt in his good hand, and his eyes were on Jimmie Judd.

"You're a nice square gent!" he said. "First scratch you get, you run to the law. I told 'em we should have left you out in the sinks with a canteen and a couple of pills."

Judd tried to bring the carbine up, but Prentiss was waiting. His .44 flashed. The Texan went back hard against the wall, and, when Grif realized his own danger, the gun had already swung to cover him. It went off—into the floor, for someone had sprung upon Prentiss from behind and pinioned his arms. Grif strode to the struggling pair and slugged the outlaw over the head with the barrel of his gun. When Prentiss slid to the floor, he saw Tom Fry behind him.

Fry looked sick. Beyond that, he was angry. "I should have known what you were dragging me into," he said. "I thought there might be trouble when I saw you come in here. So I followed. Damn you, Grif!"

Grif figured that the less Fry saw of the dead man, the better, and he said quickly: "Has this burg got a marshal?"

"Senator Montgomery is a sort of justice of the peace," Tom Fry said. "I'll get him."

Will Riordan swore when he arrived on the scene. "This is the thanks I get for trying to run a decent place," he said. "Murder!"

"What did you think was wrong with Judd?" Grif asked him. "Measles?"

"They told me his leg was broke."

"It was. By a bullet."

40

A few minutes later the senator was panting like a donkey engine in the door, staring at the man on the bed. "Jerusalem!" he said. "That can't be . . . Jimmie Judd! Why, I delivered his eulogy six months ago!"

"I guess you'll have to do it all over again," Grif said. "You'll find somebody else in his grave . . . probably a Mex or some teamster with his face caved in. I've got a hunch the man you pulled out from under the wagon was throwed there by Jimmie and his *compadres* after the so-called hold-up. You might call the picture before you . . . 'The Wages of Sin.' Jimmie was just telling me the kingpin's name when Prentiss stepped in."

The senator's wattle-like jowls quivered. "You mean, suh . . . we have the scoundrel's name at last?"

"Not quite. But it was a good miss. Have you got a room somewhere where we can bottle up this snake?"

The senator waved his hand. "Storeroom at my place. Like a safe." He shot a sharp glance at Will Riordan. "Was this man Prentiss staying here?"

"I never seen him before," Riordan said.

He looked so smug, so confident that his coattails were clean, that Grif deemed it a propitious moment for a question of his own. "Maybe you'd like to tell us why all those gun cases are being unloaded into your wine cellar?"

VII

Riordan looked blank. "Gun cases?" he said. Then he began to laugh. "You mean those boxes Sig's unloading in back? Sure, they're gun cases. I bought them at Fort Seldon . . . empty. With timber so scarce, I figured I could use them in enlarging this place."

Grif frowned, cursing silently, and went out the back, and dragged one of the narrow boxes off the pile. On the side of it was stenciled: **Colt's Patent Fire Arms Mfg. Co. Hartford, Conn.** He did not have to tear the top off to know it was empty.

"You win that hand, Riordan," he said. "Let's lock up our boy before he comes to, Senator."

He and Tom Fry carried Bud Prentiss up the street to the Wells Fargo office. The dusty little front office contained a large wooden safe with an oil painting on the front, and a roll-top desk. The walls were covered with green tin sheets that had been stamped in the semblance of bricks.

Mary Storm was sitting at the desk, working with a letter-press. She gave Grif a relieved smile when she saw him. "I was worried about you, Mister Holbrook," she told him. "I thought we'd never see you again when those outlaws took you."

"I was a little worried about me, too," Grif said. He dumped Bud Prentiss into the small, windowless room the senator indicated. Montgomery closed the door and replaced the big brass padlock.

When Grif looked around, he saw that Tom Fry had left. Mary was watching him cross the street to the hotel. "You see?" she said to Grif. "I was a fool ever to come. Nothing will change Tom unless he does it himself."

"He's got a bad case of it," Grif agreed. "But I've got some plans that may wipe the smoke off his dark glasses."

Grif took a room next to Tom Fry's in the Desert Rest. The sun sank behind the Dragoons in a brassy haze. Just after darkness took the town, Aimee Prentiss visited him.

She sat down in the chair, looking stiff and frightened.

"I lied to you, Mister Holbrook," she said. "I knew Bud was staying at the saloon. But I . . . I couldn't turn him in."

Grif kept wariness between them like a screen. She was as pretty and as treacherous as a silver-plated Derringer.

"That ain't what you came here to tell me," he said.

Aimee's violet eyes mounted to his, and faltered. "No," she admitted. "I came to warn you. They're going to try to get Bud out of the Wells Fargo office tonight."

Grif sat down, not taking his eyes from her. "How they planning to do it?"

"Three of them are going to break in after the senator goes to the hotel," Aimee said tensely. "I heard Will Moriarty talking with Johnny Burns and another man called Salty Adams."

Grif squinted across his gun barrel. "Aimee," he said, "you're a pretty little thing, but so is a sidewinder in August. John Butterfield sent me down here to bust up the ring that's wrecking the Oxbow. If I have to kill a few people to do it, that's accordin' to the book, and Butterfield didn't say anything about not killing women. I shore hope you're not double-crossing me again, like the time you sat on my lap. Because I've been in this business so long the only law I know is self-preservation."

Aimee gasped. "Oh, no! I've haven't anything to gain by lying. Even if Bud escapes, they'll kill him eventually. All I want is to see this brutal killing end."

"Did Bud ever tell you who's giving orders to the crowd?"

"I don't think he knows. None of them do . . . except Johnny Burns. And the ringleader is someone bigger than Johnny."

Grif finished cleaning the gun, reloaded it, and slung it under his arm. "I'm a fool," he said, "but I'm trusting you, Aimee. I'll be across the street from the Wells Fargo office when they come. And I'll git 'em. You just keep it under your pretty little hat, will you?"

Aimee nodded vigorously. "I will, Grif. Oh, I will."

After she had gone, Grif smiled. *You will like hell!* he thought.

He and Tom Fry ate at the lunch counter, then sought the senator, working late over his desk.

"Just in time for a smile," he said. "This blasted desert air dehydrates a man."

He poured three stiff drinks, and they sat around sipping the warm whisky. Grif went over to the wall lamp. "You object to drinkin' in the dark?" he asked.

Senator Montgomery seemed puzzled. "I don't quite understand."

"Safer. They're going to try to bust Bud Prentiss out of here tonight."

The senator set his glass down with a thump. "The blackguards," he said. "I'll see the whole pack of them locked up. How did you hear of this?"

"From Aimee Prentiss. I told her I'd be across the street, waiting. She'll pass it on to Moriarty, and they'll come a-smokin' into the alley. But I'll be right here, settin' by the safe. I'll knock 'em over like partridges as they come in the door."

Tom Fry grunted. He had brought a stage whip with him, and he sat there with it looped over his shoulder. It was his sole concession to violence.

For a moment Montgomery was silent. "Perhaps," he said, "discretion would be the better part of valor in this case. Not being much of a hand with a pistol, I shall leave the field to you."

"Might be a good idea," Grif said to Tom Fry, "if you went back to the hotel, too. I look for some unpleasantness."

Tom's tone was dogged. "I'll stay. If Moriarty and his crowd are all we have to contend with, all we'll need is a handful of buckshot."

After the senator had departed, Grif got up. He draped his coat over the back of his chair, buttoning it down the front. He made a cylinder out of the desk blotter and shoved it down the front of the coat, so that it protruded from the neck in the rough semblance of a head. Atop it he put his black, flat-crowned Stetson.

"Let's go over and wait in the alley," Grif said.

They circled by back streets to the alley across from the stage office. Fry had his whip unlimbered, in the blind hope that he might be able to take someone alive. The night was hot and still, full of small sounds and odors. There was the smell of warm, dry earth, and down the street a perfidious redhead with the face of a saint was singing a song about mother to some men who had almost forgotten they ever had one.

Grif was thinking about how a boy and a sweet girl had been dragged into a mess that sent its stink up to heaven. There was one conviction in him, and it was that a string went from this dusty little town of Dragoon, New Mexico Territory, right down to some cigar-smoke-laden office in the deep South. He could feel, like a pre-storm pressure, the boiling black clouds of war closing about them. And standing there in the darkness, Grif Holbrook sighed for a lot of kids who would be dying on battlefields instead of begetting themselves children and building the kind of businesses that bound this country together. . . .

When he saw the gunmen, they were so close that he reached out to squeeze Tom Fry's arm. They were slipping along the boardwalk across the street. If Aimee had run true to form, they would immediately turn their guns upon this alley where they stood like two erect shadows. But they didn't. One of them reached for the door of the Wells Fargo office and tried the knob. He stepped back, and very suddenly the pair stepped together to the door, slammed it open, and poured a flashing barrage of shots into the dummy before the safe.

Tom Fry and Grif stepped into the street and, just as the men stepped back, Grif spoke: "Takin' you boys, dead or alive. Your choice."

Tom's long mule-whip snaked out as one of the pair started on a sprint for the alley that flanked the stage office. The man tripped and went down, but he rolled over and came up to fire one shot and duck into the alley. Fry hauled the whip back and went after the other.

Grif was already in conference with the man. Johnny Burns, for his slender height had betrayed him, was running toward the hill-end of the street, his Colt crashing as he ran. Grif stood with his legs planted wide, pivoting smoothly to get rhythm of the man's pace. He squeezed off the shot. Burns stumbled and lurched against the adobe wall of a store. He went to his knees, then he dragged himself up and floundered on.

It was like shooting a wounded rabbit, but Grif Holbrook was recalling a ride in a certain Concord, and a stage conductor who had been shot down in cold blood. He put his next shot into the outlaw's left shoulder. Johnny Burns flung his arms before him and fell at full length.

Grif looked at Tom Fry. "How do you feel?" he asked.

Tom scratched his head, the whip hanging loosely. "Kinda . . . queasy," he said. "But, dog-gone it, Grif . . . that was almost pretty, the way you did it! Kind of . . . rhythmical. . . ."

"It's the timin'," Grif said. "Yeah, you get so a purty-placed shot is like a work of art to you. You get a little proud of your work."

Fry shook himself. "But it's not for me," he said. "If I'd killed him, I'd have two ghosts to face every night."

They approached Johnny Burns, while men ran toward the Wells Fargo office from the lower end of town. "It's too bad," Grif sighed. "You got the guts of a first-class lawman. But I guess it ain't your line. Well, you might as well go back to the hotel. I'll take care of the details."

VIII

Senator Montgomery, looking considerably rumpled, arrived after Johnny Burns had been neatly arranged on the counter, his gray eyes closed for the last time. Montgomery looked at him, his red jowls quivering, and then he turned and began to push the saloon crowd out into the street. "Get out of here!" he bellowed. "We don't need yo' help."

He shut and locked the door. He stood by the body of the young outlaw, and suddenly the stage man saw moisture in his eyes. The fat senator shuffled to the back and meaninglessly, numbly, adjusted papers on his desk.

"Senator," Grif said, "I'm sorry you couldn't have been the one to go first. It would have been easier all around."

Montgomery's cumbersome body straightened, but he did not face him. "I . . . I don't understand. . . ."

"It's hard to see a son killed," Grif said. "I don't know how I missed it for so long that Johnny Burns was really Johnny Montgomery. You've both got the deepest julep-and-cotton-plantation accents I ever did hear. And you've got the eyes. They could be nice eyes . . . if they didn't have murder in them. I hoped I could take him alive, Senator. For your sake."

The senator's head bent lower. "Yes," he said. "He was my son. You know everything except what you came to find out, don't you? Where the stages are kept."

47

"I reckon I can wring that out of one of the saloon crowd."

The senator turned. He was not smiling, and his face was like a death-cast. But it had determination and a message of danger, and not until he raised his right hand from his side did Grif realize he had let a Derringer drop into his palm from his sleeve. "We're sensible men," Montgomery said. "I'd like to kill you, but I'll forego the pleasure because I'll need some time to get out of town. We'll meet again, Holbrook. I'll see to that. Turn around."

Grif hesitated, and the man repeated the order sharply. Grif turned. He heard a key rattle in a lock, and then a door creaked, and Bud Prentiss came out of the closet. Prentiss's voice was almost hysterical. "Now, you lard-bellied four-flusher!"

An arm cast a shadow on the wall as it swung at Grif's head. He ducked, but too late to avoid the weight that sledged blindingly against his head and poured waves of hot, star-shot crimson into his brain. . . .

A series of crashing sounds levered Grif Holbrook back to consciousness. A door fell with a crash, and light struck his eyes. Tom Fry strode into the closet where Prentiss had been imprisoned. He held an axe in his hand, and he was tight-mouthed. Grif lay there on the floor, tied hand and foot and gagged. Fry cut him loose, but Grif was too sick and numb to move.

Fry saw Grif's Colt, unloaded, lying on the floor. He uncapped the canteen in the shoulder stock and held it to Grif's lips. Grif lay back, letting the raw liquor drive the shakes out of him. Fry sat on a box, rolling a cigarette, while three other men made a clatter in the outer office. "This is nice," he said. "The senator's gone. So is Will Moriarty, and Prentiss, and Salty Adams. And so," he said, after a pause, "is Mary."

Grif started up. "Mary? Where?"

Tom threw the cigarette down. His mouth was a bitter slash. "They took her," he said. "She wasn't in her room this morning, but there was a note . . . 'Try to follow us and the girl dies.' It wasn't signed."

Grif held his head in his hands. "What time is it?"

"Noon. We thought they'd taken you, too, since they took the senator."

Grif's head raised. "Ha! He took *them!* Don't you know why I sent you back to the hotel last night? Because I was going to take Montgomery prisoner, and I reckoned he'd fight. He was the boss. He knows he's milked this territory dry. Now he'll take his booty and his crowd and move on. I've failed, Tom. Failed Butterfield, and the whole country."

Tom went to the door and stood staring into the office. "Failed?" he said. "I'm the one that's failed, Grif. If I'd gone whole hog with you, we'd have cleaned the pack out. But I was too worried about my scruples and my conscience. By God, Grif, if I had a chance at them now. . . ."

Grif laid his hand on Tom's shoulder. "It takes strong medicine for strong fever. But we aren't licked yet. What's been done?"

Fry shrugged. "We trailed 'em. They rode out into the desert and split up. By the time we try to follow all of those trails, they'll be clean to California or Texas. If they hurt Mary, Grif . . . !"

Grif held his palms to his head. "Let's go over to the hotel," he said.

He spread out a Dixson and Kasson's map and traced all the likely trails. An army could spread out in a forage line twenty miles wide and never cut sign on the renegades.

Grif grunted. "I'm goin' down to the Blood Bucket and

see if I can wring anything out of the swampers," he said.

He went rough-shod through the saloon hirelings. Grif took some skin off a few noses, but he succeeded only in convincing himself that nobody knew anything. At dusk he sat on the hitch rack of the hotel, under the shade of the wide wooden awning. He wandered down to Bay-Rum Brown's and turned himself over to the Dragoon magpie for everything that could be done to the human head, short of surgery. Bay-Rum still had a breath like after-shave lotion, and he was still full of meaningless chatter.

"The works," Grif growled. "Start with a shave, and see what you can do with the rings under my eyes."

"A specialty," said Bay-Rum Brown. "I've handled the Blood Bucket trade for years."

Grif lay back, closing his eyes. Bay-Rum's conversation flowed on, and Grif was almost asleep when he heard Sig Johnson's name.

"Ol' Sig's a busy man these days," said the barber. "Hauls in town one day and the next he's hittin' the trail again. El Paso. Takin' a load of likker and groceries down, seems like. Seen him loadin' up an hour ago behind the Blood Bucket. . . . Say!" He straightened, razor held at port arms. "That sounds funny, don't it? Freightin' grub from here to El Paso!"

Grif stood up, wiping lather off his face on the polka-dot apron. "It sounds damn' funny," he said. "I think I might have a talk with Sig."

There was an alley behind the saloon from the end of which Grif could see Sig Johnson and a swamper lashing a tarpaulin across under considerable strain. Sweating, he checked the canvas and turned to his helper.

"That does 'er, George," he said. "Now, we'll bring the mules over, and I'll get started."

Grif slipped back down the alley and walked swiftly to the

hotel. He said to Tom Fry: "Buckle on your hardware, Tommy."

Fry reached for the holstered Colt. "You've found 'em?"

"Not sure yet. But we're going to find out why Sig Johnson is freightin' food and whisky *to* El Paso, just after bringin' it up."

IX

When Sig Johnson made camp far out on the desert that night, two men hunkering among boxes and barrels in his rear wagon thanked God for the end of jolting. After the camp was quiet, Grif stuck his head from under the tarp. From the stars, he found they were far south of the usual freight trail. Eastward rose the dark bulk of the Chiricahuas—the Cherrycows, to those who knew the rugged, topsy-turvy range—with a deep V slashed through the highest run of peaks.

Sometime during the morning the wagons had begun to climb. The mule-skinner had had to rest his animals frequently. Grif had stuck his head out and seen that they were in a cañon that was like a slot gouged through the mountains. They had bumbled on for another four hours. There had been a sudden cessation of movement. A man's voice had barked: "What's the word?"

The big Swede on the box had cursed. "You ought to know me by now, Chunk. The word's Savannah."

The man had called: "Sure I do. But I got orders to double check everybody. Travelin' alone?"

Johnson had popped his whip. He had said: "No. I got two regiments of cavalry under the tarp!"

Chunk had laughed. The wagons had rolled on. Soon the trail had become another, leveling off. Grif had heard voices, and the wagons had stopped.

The voice of Will Moriarty had called: "Senator'll be glad to see you, Sig. He's been havin' fits about Lard-Belly gettin' on to you."

Johnson had laughed. "I left him down at the saloon. Where's the senator?"

"In his cabin. He'll want to see us all."

Johnson had grunted as his boots hit the ground. "How's the girl taking it?"

"She's stopped fightin'. Senator's got her in his back room. He's takin' it pretty hard about Johnny. Half crazy."

Grif had felt Tom Fry writhe, and he had laid an imperative hand on his arm. Grif now ventured a glance outside. What he saw made him draw a quick breath and wriggle out from under the canvas to drop to the ground.

They were in a valley as round as a bowl, a flashing creek bisecting it and green-black stands of timber among the broken rocks of the encircling walls. Where the stream made a lazy coil in the green of the meadow, a cluster of cabins made the patterns of a tiny frontier fort. What particularly caught his eyes was a fleet of fine Concord stagecoaches.

Tom Fry jumped down beside him. Nearest them was the commissary, from which came the sounds of Johnson's voice and the laughter of other men. The bunkhouses, two of them, ranged north up the street. Grif was looking for an isolated cabin that would probably be the best building of the lot. Then, beyond the stables, he saw the arsenal.

He started to work toward the arsenal. There was no guard on the powder magazine, so they were able to reach the door without being discovered. After smashing the rusty padlock Grif slid into the musty interior. Late afternoon sunlight, slanting through the door, illuminated stacks of powder kegs and long racks of muskets. There was everything here to equip an entire regiment of mounted rifles.

"Tommy," Grif breathed, "we're going to make history."

Fry said: "One way or another. Why did you have to bust in here instead of going after Mary?"

"Ideas," Grif said. "Me bein' the one that can be trusted not to go into a clinch as soon as I see her, I'm leaving you here to do the big job. When I give you the hand signal from the senator's cabin, you come runnin'. All you got to do is run a fuse into one of them kegs long enough to burn for about five minutes. Then light 'er, and duck."

They could hear Johnson, Moriarty, and Salty Adams crossing the bare ground toward the senator's cabin. Grif let them enter the cabin before he left the magazine. A sharp and breathless pressure was on him as he walked, a heavy-shouldered figure in dusty black clothes. How the next five minutes went for a shotgun guard might determine how the future went for the Union.

Grif paused at the rear of the stable, struck a handful of friction matches, and threw them into the hay. He ran on and flattened beside the front wall of Senator Montgomery's cabin.

"There's no use waiting here until they track us down, men," the senator was saying. "I think it best to go into Mexico for a few months. Then we will begin again, possibly in the vicinity of Tucson."

Aimee Prentiss said in a thin, hard voice: "And the girl?"

"I don't know. Something will turn up."

Smoke was beginning to ooze out of the thatch-like roof of the barn. The dry hay had caught swiftly, sending up a roar as it flared out every chink and window of the big barn.

Grif gave Tom Fry the signal. He was ready when the senator threw open the door and stood in the portal, shouting: "The barn's afire, men! Get every bucket in camp and form a brigade."

Men burst out the doors of the bunkhouses, hostlers and blacksmiths and gunmen. Grif pushed the barrel of his gun into the astonished senator's ribs, driving him back into the room. Tom Fry came up, panting. They held the startled group at bay while the sounds of shouting men came into the room.

"We'd like to take you back alive," Grif told them, "but it's all up to you. Just for a few minutes we'll stay right here."

"You can't do it," the senator said. There was desperation and hatred in his cold eyes.

"I'll manage," Grif said. "What you're going to do now is lie down on your faces. Pretty soon things are going to rattle around a little, and I want to know right where you are." He said to Tom: "How long did you cut that fuse?"

"About a foot," Tom Fry said.

Grif said: "My God!" He looked out the window and saw the bucket brigade running past the powder magazine, fifteen or twenty men carrying wooden buckets. Then he saw the whole line jerk, as if yanked off balance by a rope. Dust devils whirled around them, around the powder magazine, while the cabin shook to a low roar. Then the main blast came.

He had counted on their being badly stunned while they worked at the barn. He had not dared to try to time the blast for a massacre, but that was what was going on before his eyes. He was conscious of the cabin's shaking, of being hurled off his feet, but before he fell, he saw a great mushroom of flame lift the roof off the arsenal and overflow the sod walls, sweeping across the ground in a pale orange cataract that killed everything it touched. He could feel the heat of it, and then the roar came, like the beating of giant kettledrums.

He lay there, stunned, hearing the sighing of wind rushing back to fill the vacuum created by the explosion. There was movement among the outlaws, and every one of the five was armed. He looked for Tom. The younger man was already on his knees with his rifle at his shoulder, and he was shouting at the senator, who lay on his belly by the door.

"Drop it!" he said.

In the Alabaman's hands the little silver Derringer sparkled. He had it trained on Grif, and he was bracing his wrist with his left hand. Time was a thread about to break, and Grif knew he could not fire before the Southerner got off his shot. He relied on Tom Fry's steady nerves to take care of the renegade king. He heard the shots as he swung to cover Salty Adams, and out of the corner of his eye he saw Senator Montgomery drop his gun and cover his face with his hands.

Adams, the chunky gunfighter with the magnificent red sideburns, was on his knees, staring at Grif over the sights of a .36 caliber Navy gun. Grif's shot punched a hole in the man's throat.

There was movement toward the rear door. Bud Prentiss and his flame-haired wife were already at the door when Grif brought Prentiss under the bore of the Dragoon pistol. Prentiss pivoted, pouring two shots at him; one of them slugged Grif heavily in the ribs. Grif went to his knees, his finger already squeezing off a round when shock struck at him. Aimee was doing the first unselfish thing Grif had ever seen her do. She was flinging herself before her husband with the blind hope of taking the shot meant for him.

It was too late to stop the shot. The hammer dropped, and Grif saw her hand go to her breast, while the red patch of her mouth distorted. Prentiss grabbed the girl and tried to use her as a shield, and perhaps it was that move which caused Grif Holbrook to bring the gun up again and place a slug in the center of the ruggedly handsome face.

There were still the saloon man and Sig Johnson to be taken care of. Turning, Grif saw that Tom Fry had already disposed of the pair. The rifle was hot and smoking, and Tom had a look on his face to match it. There would be no more nights when the ghosts of dead men stood about his head. . . .

They found Mary Storm unharmed in the bedroom. Grif choked a little when he saw the girl's arm go about Fry's neck. This was something he would never have, this tenderness that only a woman could bring into a man's life.

They went outside and hitched up a team for a Concord. Then Tom Fry and Grif rounded up the wounded men and stowed them as best they could in the boot and interior of the stagecoach for the long trip to Dragoon. When they started out, Grif held the ribbons, and Mary sat between him and Tom.

Grif said: "I reckon you've got a job with Butterfield as long as you want it, Tom. You're the kind of stage man the Oxbow needs."

Tom shook his head. It was sundown; the air was cool, and he had his arm about a slim waist, and for the first time in many months the shadows were gone from his eyes. "No," he said. "It's Tennessee for us. There's war comin', Grif. When it comes, Mary and I belong with the South. A man's got to live accordin' to his lights."

They passed the spot where Chunk had been, but he was gone. The stagecoach rolled out onto the flat face of the desert just at moonrise. Tom Fry and the girl were silent, filled with their own thoughts.

There was something very sad about it all, for Grif, and it brought a wave of self-pity over him. Everybody had won but him, who had done the most. It didn't seem fair. Then he sighed, and, clucking up the leaders, he leaned back with his foot on the brake.

Ah, well. There was something in being a free agent. The

world was big and bright, and who knew? Maybe there was a red-headed widder just around the corner waiting for him. . . .

Bullets Blaze the Stage Trails

I

The civilian doctor pressed his lips tightly together and brought the war point out of the wound with his tweezers. The man in the operating chair swore and took another pull at a bottle of brandy.

"Crow, ain't it?" the doctor said. He held the arrowhead in the sunlight falling obliquely through a window.

Grif Holbrook said: "Sioux."

"It's getting," said the doctor, "so a man can say . . . 'I was over the Sweetwater trail,' just like he'd brag he was at Antietam."

"Only they don't give battle ribbons," Grif remarked. He winced as the doctor began to clean and dress the wound. He watched the gauze go tightly around his thigh, and then he stood up and tested his leg. He wiped the arrowhead on his pants and dropped it in his pocket. "Send the bill to John Butterfield," he told the doctor.

The doctor looked at him curiously. "Haven't you heard the news?" he asked.

Grif was tired and half-starved; he had looked into death's eye sockets today, and he was still shaky. He had a short answer on his tongue, and then, suddenly, he knew what the doctor meant. "Butterfield's gone under?" he said.

"That's what they tell me. Ben Holladay came in last night. I understand he's foreclosed on him. He owns the

58

whole kit and caboodle . . . every wagon and mule of the Great Central Overland."

Emotion worked slowly to the surface in Grif Holbrook. It was something he could not grasp immediately. He had been with John Butterfield for twelve years; he and his half-breed Colt had taken the stage czar's part in a score of minor wars. He was on Butterfield's payroll, but it wasn't as though Butterfield were his boss. They were partners, even though Grif had nothing invested in the firm but loyalty.

He paid the doctor and went out. A ferret-toothed wind was whooping along the street, sharpened by the frosty whetstones of the Rockies. The frozen mud had been ground into mush by the hoofs of cavalry and the wagons slogging through Fort Sanders this busy spring of 1863.

He limped on, grumbling about the cold, a bearish man with Stetson pulled low and coat collar turned up. He didn't like this northern country. He remembered the old days of the Great Southern Overland in Texas and New Mexico, before the war had forced Butterfield to move the line north. Trouble had been their portion ever since.

Sioux and road agents had shredded the fiber of the Wyoming division of the road until only a rotten thread remained. For months Grif Holbrook had tried to convince Butterfield that his place was down in Virginia, fighting with the Army of the Potomac, but all the stage man could understand was that, if Grif deserted him, the whole line would fall apart. Just knowing the veteran shotgun guard was up there on the box was enough to discourage some ambitious road agents. And now Grif had his chance, but he felt no gratification, only a grayness in him at the realization that all he and Butterfield had been so long in building up had been pushed over by the hand of Holladay, the capitalist.

At the stage station, the stationmaster was gloomily packing his belongings. "Holladay's at Hall's Hotel," he said. "Wants to see you."

"I'd like to see him, too," said Grif, "in hell! What are you packing for?"

"I reckon we're all fired," said the other. "If we ain't, me and the boys are quitting anyway. We're all going over to the fort in the morning to join up."

Grif said: "You'll wait for me, sonny! Two years I've been aching to get in, and I ain't standing at the end of a line now."

It was the one bright spot in the picture. The war that had been going to end in three months still dragged on. Grif Holbrook knew that what the Army of the Potomac needed was a certain bull-hided old shotgun messenger who could tell a few generals something about fighting.

From the fort came the sweet, sharp notes of "Recall," and Grif was suddenly homesick—homesick for discomfort and hunger and the rough camaraderie of the infantry. Not since the Mexican War, in 1848, had he tasted the flavor of war, and now he wanted it desperately.

He called on Ben Holladay that night, just to see whether he was worth taking a poke at. He couldn't hit an old man, of course, but maybe he could hang him from a wall hook. He had his eyes set for a man about five-eight, but when the door opened, he was looking at Ben Holladay's ruby-and-diamond shirt studs. About a foot above was the man's face— black-bearded, hawk-nosed, fierce-eyed.

"Come in," Holladay commanded. "Set down. Have a drink."

Grif was too taken aback to refuse. Holladay poured liquor in thick glass tumblers. He watched Grif sample his. "Corn likker." He grinned. "I have it sent from Missouri. Costs like champagne, tastes a sight better. I was weaned on it." He kept on his feet, moving restlessly about. He seemed compelled to shout everything he said.

Grif was remembering all the things he'd heard about the man. That he had a palace on the Hudson that had cost over a million dollars, that he had a finger in half the industries in the country. But Holladay, to him, had the smell of a Missouri farmer.

Grif said: "So you cut John Butterfield's throat."

Holladay clasped his hands behind him, fastening those black agate eyes on the shotgun messenger. "That's the way," he said. "Trot out your grievances and we'll thresh 'em out. No, I didn't cut his throat. At the last, he didn't own more than a tenth of the Great Central Overland. He was smart enough to begin unloading stock a year ago. His partners were blocking every move he made to improve the service. He was ready to quit."

"I still took orders from him," Grif growled.

"Nominally. I bought the firm out because the country needs a stage line, and I happened to need a good investment."

Grif's grin had malice in it. "You'd make more money selling Union flags in Richmond," he said. "Why, the Sweetwater Division is as good as done. Between outlaws and Injuns, a man's life ain't worth nine cents between here and Green River."

"I'm not worried about the Sweetwater," Ben Holladay stated. "I've already arranged with the President for troops to patrol it. The California division has me thinkin' . . . ."

Grif started. "Not for ten thousand dollars!" he vowed. "Me and staging are quits. Tomorrow I go back into the infantry. And damn glad of it."

Ben Holladay could throw words like rocks. "So you're quitting!"

Grif stabbed a finger at Holladay. "Don't start fiddlin'

that string, brother! I had to be patriotic and stay in staging, before. This time I'm being patriotic and gettin' out."

"Of course you ain't interested," Holladay said, "but I'll straighten you out on why I need you. You're going as my ambassador. From Carson City to Placerville, the Overland belongs to two independent lines Butterfield was never able to buy out. We pay tribute for the privilege of going over these jerk-line outfits. We lose money for every passenger we take through. All I want you to do is find out why they won't sell . . . and make 'em."

Grif Holbrook finished his drink. "Good likker," he said, wiping his mouth. "But damn' poor company." He stood up. From the doorway, he gave Holladay a mock salute. "See you in Richmond, sonny. Me and staging have forgot all about each other."

Overnight, all the stage crowd except Grif changed their minds about joining the Army. The stationmaster sheepishly confessed they had succumbed to fifty percent raises over a bottle of corn whisky. In high disgust, Grif stalked out into the bitterly bleak and cold morning.

He walked up to the fort. His joints were stiff; the wound in his leg ached dully. Wyoming was making an old man out of him.

The only thing he liked about Holladay's offer was the California angle. They said you rode in your shirt sleeves all winter out there. Grif had a pile of gold pieces saved up for the California cattle ranch he was going to buy someday; in his wallet he carried a diamond ring he was going to slip on the finger of the first red-headed widder he met when he reached the Coast.

In the adjutant's office a fire burned ruddily on the hearth. The adjutant looked at Grif's warrant and sent an orderly for the post surgeon. Grif had the feeling, as he stripped to his waist, that the officers were smiling at him. He had to admit he looked pretty white, but he was as hard as granite all through. He kept his chest out and his stomach sucked in.

Captain Carruthers, the surgeon, went through the routine of pounding and measuring. "You'd do for a draft horse, Holbrook," he said. "Now, let's see you jump up and down about fifty times. First one leg and then the other."

Grif jumped once; his bad leg caved in, and down he went. He got up red-faced. "Got a little Charley horse in that left leg," he admitted. "Arrer wound. Be all right in a week."

The surgeon stroked his chin. "We can't take you, of course, until it's healed. Come around again in about six months."

Grif let out a bellow. "Six months! Damn it!" he said. "I'll take on the stoutest dogface in the fort right now! I'll show all of you some tricks about soldiering."

Captain Carruthers smiled. "I'm sorry. ARs, you know."

Army Regulations! There were tears of fury in Grif's eyes as he dressed. It was not until he was at the bottom of the hill that he discovered the thick envelope in his coat pocket. With the wind flapping at the pages, he stood there and read Ben Holladay's letter. Now he knew why the officers had grinned at him.

> This looked the only way, Grif. The way I see it, you're trying to get out of finishing a job you started years ago, with Butterfield . . . linking the nation by good roads, so that a man don't have to be a pioneer to cross a county line. Take the night stage. Attached is a list of your duties, information, etc.
>
> B.H.

As simple as that. If you had influence, you could do anything. Grif unslung the half-breed Dragoon Colt he carried under his shoulder, the .44 with the rifle stock and revolver frame. He removed a plug from the shoulder plate and drank noisily of the liquid gunpowder he carried in the weapon's walnut bosom. Fortified, he went back to town and packed.

Holladay had him on the ropes. Maybe his conscience had been needling him just a bit, too. The Army wouldn't have him, and he sure wasn't ready to retire. So it was California, and more grief.

He discarded all of his long-handled underwear except one pair to wear on the trip. He took one woolen shirt. In California they'd laugh at him if he came dressed like an Eskimo.

He had three hours to wait for the stage. He reread the attachment to Holladay's letter, and got mad again when he discovered that he would have a confederate out there: Buckskin Johnny Bullis! What kind of shenanigan was this? Everybody knew Bullis. He was a killer, a no-good, whisky-drinking product of the gold camps. Bullis would take charge of the California section as division agent. He would meet Grif at Placerville, and they would sweat through the job together.

"Call to Quarters" sounded nostalgically from the fort as the stage whirled out of town, and Grif Holbrook's eyes were misty with longing. He buried his nose in the buffalo robe and tried to sleep.

II

This time the stage rattled through the Sweetwater country unmolested. At Salt Lake City, all the passengers except Grif

Holbrook disembarked. A few more travelers boarded the mail coach. As he watched the hostlers back a fresh team into the breeching, Grif noticed a man standing beside him. The stranger was a stocky, sandy-haired Army major, wearing a light blue uniform with the bright yellow slashes of the cavalry. He appeared young for his rank, but he had a fighter's jaw and a look of capability.

"You're Holbrook?" the major asked Grif.

Grif frowned. "Now, don't tell me you're Buckskin Johnny Bullis!"

"Stubbs," the officer said. "Major Adam Stubbs. Holladay didn't tell you about me, just as a matter of precaution. I'll be working with you. I'm taking over a company of volunteers at Cold Springs station, to patrol the route."

"What's Holladay think I am?" Grif demanded. "A cripple? I used to be able to take care of myself."

Stubbs sounded as though the job was not something he had asked for, either. "I don't know whether this gang of men will be taking care of us, or we'll be taking care of them. I've never seen them. They're volunteers . . . probably think the Manual of Arms is a book. Dammit," he said, "I had a pretty good outfit in the Sixth."

Grif put out his hand. "Shake on it, Major. I've been trying to get back in the infantry for three years myself. What do you know about this deal?"

"Not much," said Stubbs. "There's two links we're supposed to take over between Carson City and Placerville. The Mountain Express Line is eighty miles long, owned by an old battle-axe known as Annie Benson. The last fifteen miles into Placerville is owned by a Banjo Harris. The Benson woman has turned down twenty thousand dollars for her lay-out. Harris refused ten. God knows why! It will take them years to make as much on tolls."

Grif climbed into the stagecoach and slumped in the seat. He said: "By God, I'll find out why!"

At Carson City, the air was warm, the desert sweet with sage. Grif expanded his lungs like a bellows. He discarded his heavy underwear and his last woolen shirt. As they pulled out, he saluted the blue Sierra Nevada, standing tall before them. "California, here I come!"

A tollgate stopped them at the foot of the grade. The passengers, getting out to stretch, were met by a tall bone-rack of a man with bristling chin whiskers and a fiery eye. His forehead was lofty, his thinning hair steel gray; he had the voice of a prophet right out of the Old Testament.

"Have you a mind to save a dollar, good friends?" he challenged.

A boot drummer asked: "What's the game, uncle . . . shells and pea?"

The man waved his hand at a battered mud wagon standing some distance away on a high-centered desert trail that ran off at an angle to the main road. "I am the proprietor of the Pioneer Shortline," he stated. "To go farther on the Great Overland means needless danger from highwaymen. I charge only twenty-five dollars to Placerville, taking the north trail around the lake. Far cheaper, in the long run."

"What makes your road safer?" Grif asked him.

"God is at the right hand of those who ride my wagons," declared the bearded one. "The Great Overland is run by ungodly men."

The operator of the tollgate called impatiently from the tollhouse: "Get it over, Hellfire! Give them the tracts and let 'em go."

Hellfire had a cold eye and a muttered reply for the man. He gave each of the passengers a pamphlet. "Then make your peace with the Lord," he rumbled.

Grif read the boldface lettering on the tract. **Get Right With God.**

The prophet returned to his stagecoach, whipped up the bony team, and rolled toward the mountain. The toll collector chuckled. "Hellfire Galvin ain't had a passenger in six months, but he ain't discouraged. He's happy just so he's spreadin' the Word."

They began to climb. Gradually Grif sensed a vague discomfort. It was getting cold. It was not even three o'clock, but the wind that whooped through the stage had sharpened its teeth on glaciers. The higher they climbed, the colder it got. By the time they reached the summit, Grif's teeth were chattering. The mountain had its cold feet on his back.

He said to Major Stubbs: "Don't look now, but are we back in Wyoming?"

"Gets pretty cold in the mountains," Stubbs told him. "Hit forty below at Emigrant Gap last winter, so they tell me."

Grif stared bitter-eyed at the green-black stands of fir and pine rushing past, his lips blue. California! You could have his share for one acre of Texas bottomland.

Dusk settled somberly over the mountains. It was, the driver calculated, about five miles to Cold Springs station. The stage lurched along a goat path blasted into a cañon side a few hundred feet above a frozen creek. The forest was brown and green and white, with an occasional scarlet flash of snow flowers.

Grif was trying to get his head under a buffalo robe when the driver's shout brought him up straight. Rifles cracked above the drumming of the horses' hoofs. The smooth run of the stage broke; the passengers were thrown in a heap on the floor. Grif dragged his Dragoon pistol out and crowded to a window.

For the first time, he saw how things were. The horses were down, struggling in the traces; the driver and guard were silent. The stagecoach was slowly sliding over the edge of the road.

After that it was one of those running nightmares in which things loom up horribly and disappear, and other things more horrible take their place. The stage was rolling with great, ungainly bounds down the hill. Grif saw one of the passengers fall half out of a window. The next time he saw him his head had been crushed. There was a crash of splintering panels, a terrific jolt that brought Grif up and banged his head on the ceiling. Then he lost consciousness.

Adam Stubbs's voice seemed to come through layers of cotton wool. "Take 'er easy, old-timer. Have a drink of this."

Grif sat up with the officer's help. He was seated on a buffalo robe, with another robe over him. Two other men lay nearby, but they had not been covered because they would not need warmth any more. The stagecoach lay, a crumpled wreck, in the stream bed.

Over the mountains night had gathered heavily. There was no sound but the wind in the crowns of the pines.

"Who were they?" Grif asked.

"I haven't seen them," Major Stubbs said "Reckon they accomplished what they set out to. The driver and guard were both shot through the head. The other two passengers are dead. When you're ready, we'll hike back up to the road and start for the station."

Grunting, his body a pattern of misery, Grif Holbrook got up, arranged the buffalo robe about him, and started up the hill. The cold came through the seams of his clothing, percolated through every pore to congeal his marrow. They plodded down the frozen stage trail.

"I'm thinking about that old duck at the foot of the grade," Grif muttered. "Hellfire Galvin. I wonder if he had the savvy to pull a play like this."

Stubbs said: "I reckon the Ten Commandments would stop him if he did have. He don't need business that bad."

They rounded a turn. Below them the forest opened up into a wide mountain park. An ocean of timber lapped at the shores of a meadow. At the far end of the meadow a collection of cabins stood in a clearing, lights shining in the windows of the main building.

Darkness was complete long before they gained Cold Springs. Dogs heralded them; the door opened, and a man stepped outside with a rifle in his hands.

"Friends!" Grif called.

"You come mighty quiet to be friends," said the station tender.

"The stage was wrecked, driver and guard killed. Are you going to let us in, or keep us freezin' out here?"

He heard women's voices. This was the station run by the woman named Annie Benson. *She better not make any trouble tonight*, thought Grif. *She better walk light and easy.*

The man stood aside for them, his jaw jutting, eyes suspicious. Grif dropped his robe on the floor and marched to the stone fireplace. He let the searing heat of the fire cook his face and thighs and shins; he thawed his frozen fingers. He took a deep breath and said: "Somebody pour me some coffee."

Someone set a big stone cup of hot coffee on the mantel before him. Grif unslung his shoulder gun, pulled out the stopper, and added a half inch of brandy to the drink. He drank it scalding, felt it sinking through him like a hot rock through snow.

Stubbs was telling the Benson woman about the wreck. She said in a tired voice: "I've been afraid something of the like was coming. I had hoped the Army troops might forestall it."

Grif said: "Do you think Ben Holladay had it done?" He turned to see the effect on her. But he was too startled at what he saw himself to observe how it affected Annie Benson.

Battle-axe—Stubbs's words rose up to mock him. Annie Benson was a small, slender woman who appeared to be in her early thirties. He wouldn't have called her pretty; handsome was a better word, for hers was a mature beauty. Her hair glistened with coppery lights, a rich auburn the color of mountain mahogany. It was parted in the middle and brushed smoothly back to each side.

Annie Benson said: "Who is Ben Holladay?"

"He closed on Butterfield last month," Grif told her. "He owns the Great Overland now." He stood there, staring like a schoolboy.

"How do you happen to know that?" the Benson woman asked him. She had quick blue eyes that watched a man's face when he spoke.

Grif was in no condition to talk business. "We'll get to that," he said.

A girl who stood near Annie Benson said: "I think what our friends need, Mother, is a hot meal and some sleep."

"Of course." The woman swung a kettle of stew out over the fire on a crane, while her daughter set two places at a table.

With hot food easing his multiple aches and pains, Grif Holbrook felt his senses dulling with fatigue.

He heard Major Adam Stubbs ask Annie Benson: "Where are these troops you mentioned?"

"Why, I wouldn't exactly know," she replied. "A Major Adam Stubbs took charge of them a few days ago. They rode south to hunt guerrillas. I haven't heard from them since."

Adam Stubbs looked as though he had been sandbagged. He blinked; his jaw went loose. But when he recovered, he did not explode into useless anger. He said to Grif: "I reckon this is our cue to turn in, pardner. We're had enough grief for today."

In the morning, Grif Holbrook got the picture of the set-up at Cold Springs station. Annie Benson, a widow for eight years, owned the Mountain Express Line. Sam Doniphan, the heavy-witted man who had challenged Grif and the major the night before, was her superintendent and man-of-all-work.

Jenny Benson, the widow's daughter, was a blonde, vivacious girl who did not seem to fit easily into the pattern of an isolated place like Cold Springs. Stubbs's eyes kept following her as she moved about the room in the morning; he had some unmilitary grins when she talked with him, and at these times the girl's cheeks always seemed unusually warm.

Stubbs asked the widow about the pseudo-Major Stubbs who had stolen his company of volunteers.

Annie said: "He was about six feet tall, I should think, thin and dark. He came in from Placerville. He said he was taking the company over, and thanked me for letting the men camp in the meadow. That was ten days ago."

"I'll be blasted if I'll let anybody steal my command," Stubbs declared. "I'll track them to hell if I have to. Have you a horse you'll sell me?"

"I have one you can use."

Every time Grif looked at the Widow Benson he thought of the diamond ring in his pocket. She looked hardly more than a girl herself, but here she was with a grown daughter. When she went out to draw water, he hurried after her to carry the buckets.

"This is a lonesome place for a widder woman," he told her. "Don't you ever think of marrying?"

Annie Benson sat beside him on the stone rim of the well. There was a scent of lavender sachet about her that was clean and fresh. "I am happy just as I am," she told him.

"You do right well here, I reckon," Grif admitted. "I suppose your husband left you the outfit?"

"My husband," Annie Benson said shortly, "left me with an eight-year-old daughter. I bought the stage line with some money from my father's estate. Don't talk to me about the advantages of marrying, Mister Holbrook."

Grif left her coldness go into him like a knife. He dropped the subject. He said: "I'll tell you why I'm here, Missus Benson. Ben Holladay sent me out to buy your stage line."

"It's not for sale," Annie declared.

"You were offered twenty thousand for your lay-out. The price is twenty-five, now."

"It still isn't for sale." Annie Benson regarded Grif shrewdly for a moment. "You look like an honest man, Mister Holbrook. Maybe you realize that I'm an honest woman. I'm not trying to hold anybody up. The Bible says . . . 'Hold fast that which is good.' This stage line is good. It was good even during the hard times of 'Fifty-Seven. Someday the Union Pacific Railroad will come through here, and I'll be paid richly for my investment."

"There's another angle, too," Grif pointed out. "The Union needs a through line to Sacramento, without toll stops and toll charges. You can do the country good. . . ."

"Then the country can pay me," said the widow. She turned her back on him and returned to the house.

Major Stubbs drew a rough map of the country from what Doniphan and the women could tell him. He put his finger on a point ten miles southwest of the station. "This Crocker Ranch," he said. "Is it big?"

Jenny Benson nodded. "The biggest in the county. Will Crocker runs ten thousand cattle. He's got a regular castle up on a bluff."

Sam Doniphan winked at the man. "And he'd shore like a queen fer that castle!"

Jenny blushed. There was the long blast of a stage horn from the road. Through the window Grif could see a low-slung mud wagon, drawn by four mules, roll into the yard. He was able to read yellow printing through the dust on the panels:

GREAT CALIFORNIA SUMMIT STAGE LINE

The coach was empty. The driver came in. He said: "Howdy, folks! What's the good word, widder?"

"The word's not good, Banjo," said Annie Benson. "These men were on a Butterfield stage that was attacked last night. They were the only survivors."

Banjo Harris clucked. "Damn the hydrophobic skunks that done it! Excuse my French . . . but if it gets much worse, I'm of a mind to sell out."

"Why not sell out before it gets worse?" Grif inquired. "I'm out here for the new operators of the Great Central Overland. I'll pay you cash for your line, Harris."

Banjo Harris was a corpulent man with a garland of red hair that went around his head like a buggy fringe, a man with blunt Gaelic features and stubbornness in the clamp of his jaws.

"Sell out?" he repeated. "Sure, I'll sell. But it'll cost you money, mister. Forty thousand."

Grif grunted. "That's nearly three thousand a mile. We

could build a detour around you for less than that."

Harris winked at Annie Benson. "You just do that," he said. "Only you'll find your detour will take you clear to Yosemite. Up here, it ain't every mountain you can build a road on."

Grif knew it, and he had no answer for the stage man. He was increasingly disgusted that he had let Ben Holladay engineer him into this whirlpool of murder and greed. He learned from Harris that he ran the stagecoach from Rimrock station to Cold Springs twice a week, in order to retain his franchise, although he seldom had a passenger.

He told Banjo Harris: "I've got to meet a man in Placerville. Are you going down today?"

"Twenty-five dollars is the price," Harris said.

Sourly Grif said: "Maybe I can do you a good turn, too, someday."

Before he left, he spoke to the widow. "I'll be back, Annie Benson," he promised. "I don't give up quick. I've got to meet Buckskin Johnny Bullis down the hill. He's the new division agent. That should show you that Ben Holladay is playing to win, this time."

Annie Benson did not move, did not make a sound, but her face had altered. There was less color in her lips, a pinched look to her eyes. She said: "If you bring Johnny Bullis up here, I'll . . . I'll run you both out with a shotgun!"

Grif studied her. "Bullis is a killer," he admitted, "but I don't reckon he makes war on widders. Besides," he added, "I've got some persuadin' ways with gunslingers myself."

Annie Benson repeated: "If you bring him up here, I'll kill him!"

On the way down Grif could not get the woman's terrified eyes out of his mind. Why was the Benson widow afraid of an ordinary gold-camp hoodlum? Maybe if she were a man, she'd have cause to fear Buckskin Johnny's famous .44. But not even a gunman would try any of his tricks on a woman.

About midday they reached Placerville, a bustling town that followed the convolutions of Hangtown Creek down a timbered slot of the hills. Now a mature settlement of fifteen years, Placerville was replacing its first hasty buildings with solid brick structures like the new Methodist church and the vainglorious Placerville Academy up on the hillside.

There were patches of snow on the hills, but the air was warm. Grif Holbrook, thinking about the bitter nights, found a dry goods store and bought a heavy suit of long underwear. Then he went on down the street to the stage office.

The stationmaster said: "Bullis? He's been waitin' for you for two weeks. You'll probably find him in the Miners' Bar. Maybe he's still sober. It's only noon."

A miner pointed out Buckskin Johnny Bullis. Bullis occupied a table in the back of the saloon. He was with a black-haired girl who wore an eyebrow-raising dance costume. They were drinking beer; the new division agent was telling a story that caused the girl to laugh. They both looked up quickly when Grif arrived.

Bullis said: "What's on your mind?" He was a rugged-looking Irishman with black, curly hair touched at the temples with gray, with blue eyes and bone-white teeth, and recklessness in the very fiber of him. Black Irish, thought Grif, and the blackness went clear to his heart, by the stories he had heard.

Grif introduced himself.

"Been looking for you," Johnny Bullis said. He patted the girl's hand. "I'll see you tonight, honey. I've got business with Grif."

Grif sat down.

"Anything new up the line?" Bullis asked him.

"Nobody's interested in selling," Grif said.

Buckskin Johnny made circles on the table top with the bottom of his beer mug. "Did the Widow Benson give you any encouragement?"

He was waiting closely for his reply, Grif thought. He was interested in Annie Benson, just as Annie had shown a negative interest in him. "She said something that might interest you," Grif told him. "She said that, if I brought you up there, she'd run us both out with a shotgun. I wonder what she could've meant?"

Bullis laughed heartily, striking the table with his fist. "Good old Annie!" he said. "She ain't changed a bit."

Grif had a sinking feeling of having reached for a step that wasn't there. "I didn't know you knew her," he said.

"Know her?" Bullis repeated. He took a faded photograph from his wallet. It could have been Jenny Benson, with a child on her lap, but it was Annie, when she had been Jenny's age. "Annie Benson," Buckskin Johnny Bullis said, "happens to be a good friend of mine. I thought I knew her when I saw her in town the other day, and I was damned sure she knew me, by the way she stared. As a matter of fact, Grif," he said, "Annie Benson happens to be my wife."

III

Grif wanted to wipe Bullis's grin away with his fist. He wanted to smash that lying mouth. He held onto the edge of the table and said: "Annie Benson's husband is dead."

Bullis leaned back, hooking his thumbs under his gun belt; he wore a single revolver, a bone-handled Navy pistol. He was seeing Grif's consternation and interpreting it correctly.

"Is that the story she gave you?" he remarked. "Well, I remember it a little different. I remember her drawing all the money I had out of the bank while I was away on a business trip. That was back in Texas. When I came home, she and the kid and the money were gone, and all I had was a letter saying *adiós*. Later on, I changed my name for business reasons."

There was an ugliness in Grif that had to come out in action. His hand knocked Bullis's beer glass off the table. He said: "You're a damned liar, Bullis. You're going to give me the straight of that story, or I'll ride you out of town on the barrel of my gun."

He was dealing with a man who was steel to the core, with a man who had fought the toughest, and lived to brag about it. Bullis's pose did not change, but his eyes darkened.

He said: "It sounds like we might have a little unpleasantness, Holbrook."

"I hope so," Grif said. "I thought Holladay was crazy when he hired a cheap gunslinger to ramrod the California division. I'm taking it on myself to fire you as of right now. But I still want an apology."

Bullis said: "You want to know about Annie. All right, here's what Annie meant to me . . . I married her as a good woman who'd make me a home and bring up my kids. What I got was a tramp . . . a thieving tramp."

Grif's foot kicked the leg of Bullis's chair, and it went over backwards. Bullis landed hard, without a sound, and rolled away. He came up on his knees, his hand pulling his gun, his finger on the trigger. Grif had the stock of his half-breed Colt against his shoulder; his thumb was on the trigger. Bullis must have known that he was crying for an excuse to fire, for he let his pistol drop.

"You're calling the figures," he said. "What's your game . . . widow-making?"

"I think I savvy how you happen to be in on this deal," Grif stated. "Now that Annie's doing all right, you'd like to cut yourself in for a share. You'd take everything she has and run out on her again. But you aren't going to, Bullis, because you're leaving town today."

Bullis stood up. He was sweating. He was counted a dangerous man, but this uncurried old shotgun guard was talking to him as though he were a drunk he was bouncing out of a saloon. "You think I am, eh?" Bullis said.

Grif yanked Buckskin Johnny's gun from the holster. "I think you better not be here after the stage leaves," he said.

He left the gun on the bar as he went outside.

California, and his red-headed widder. . . . Yesterday he had thought he had both. He'd finish this job quick, buy a ranch—on the desert, where it was warm—and dedicate the next few months of his life to talking the Widow Benson into remarrying. And now the widow had a husband. A cheap gold-camp killer. A loose-talking cull.

Grif had some old-fashioned ideas about chivalry. They didn't condone deserting families. They didn't forgive loose remarks about women.

The diamond ring in his pocket seemed as heavy as a horseshoe and, to him, as worthless.

Joel Fergus sat in his cage in the rear of the Placerville Bank like a slightly seedy buzzard. He was a leathery little man with a wrinkled face and a neck like a turkey gobbler. Grif showed him Ben Holladay's letter of credit.

Fergus studied the signature. "Fifteen thousand!" he said. "All right, you can draw on it whenever you like. Anything else?"

Grif tried to sound professional, but guilt oozed out. "About this Annie Benson . . . is her title to the Mountain

Express Line clear?"

"Far as I know," Fergus grunted.

"I mean," Grif said, "did she buy it outright, or might there be a loan against it somewhere?"

"She paid cash. Matter of fact," Fergus said, his rusty-nail voice warming, "she bought it on my advice. That was in 'Fifty-Six, seven years ago. She'd been a widow just a year . . . came out here for a change of scenery. Her father left her some money, and she asked my advice about investing it."

Grif asked the question he was almost afraid of. "She paid cash . . . hard dollars, eh?"

Fergus moved some papers on his desk. "Well, no. She had title to her father's ranch, in Texas. I took care of selling it and reinvesting."

Grif took a deep breath. The sun came through the windows a little brighter; the air was sweet. Annie Benson had told the truth.

Fergus was looking past him. A pinch, which might have been worry, came between his eyes. Grif Holbrook, following his glance, saw at one of the wickets the long-shanked proprietor of the Pioneer Shortline—Job Galvin. Hellfire Galvin, with his pockets bulging with religious tracts and his wiry gray head hatless.

"You were in a little accident the other night," Fergus said. "Don't think such accidents will be over the day you buy out Annie Benson and Banjo Harris. They may just be starting."

He pulled out a lower drawer and found a pamphlet that at first glance looked like the treatise Grif had been given. But Joel Fergus dropped his voice when he showed it to Grif.

"Bear Flaggers's propaganda," he said. "Ever heard of 'em? There's plenty around. They think it would be nice if California seceded from the Union and set up a Bear Flag Republic. They think right now would be a good time to do it, with the war on. I found that on the floor of Galvin's stage-coach one day when he drove me up to Auburn. You're the first I've showed it to."

Grif was thinking about Adam Stubbs's stolen battalion. "What's his game?"

"Maybe he's trying to raise an army. There's another man I'm wondering about, too . . . Will Crocker."

"The rancher?"

Fergus nodded. "He's a big man. The wealthiest in the county, but maybe that ain't enough for him. Maybe he'd like to ride into the capital on the Bear Flag Rebellion and have his pick of appropriated ranches and God knows what. Galvin comes in here every month with a check of Crocker's and cashes it . . . takes the cash up to Crocker's ranch. I don't know what Crocker wants with cash 'way out there." He added hurriedly: "Put that pamphlet in your pocket. Here's Galvin."

Galvin's eyes showed no recollection of Grif Holbrook. He laid a check before the banker.

"Your approval is required," he said.

He was a strange character, Grif thought. Not of this world—he didn't see you when he looked at you. He lived in a rarified atmosphere of long-haired principles and crazy ideas. But there was something in the matter of that Bear Flag pam-phlet that made him more mundane. Prophet or traitor, he was grinding an axe.

"Three thousand," Fergus remarked. "You think it's safe to carry that much cash?"

Galvin said: "Will Crocker's worry. I'm taking it up to him. If I'm robbed, it's his look-out."

Grif Holbrook said: "Maybe I could ride up with you, Galvin. I've got business with him."

Galvin's yellow hawk's eyes came down to Grif's level. "A dollar fifty a mile," he declared. "Eighteen dollars. I have to pay that blackguard, Harris, five dollars toll."

If it went on much longer, Grif thought, he'd spend the whole fifteen thousand in tolls. "When do you leave?"

Hellfire Galvin said: "Four o'clock."

The afternoon stage from Carson City rolled in, changed teams, and departed for Sacramento, in the valley. Grif Holbrook was at the stage station when it left, but Buckskin Johnny Bullis was not aboard.

Grif checked the loads of his gun; it was awkward to discover, when you pulled the trigger, that a cap had worked off the nipple. He permitted himself the smidgeon of comfort from the canteen in the stock of his Colt. In his stomach there was a coldness. He was not actually afraid of Bullis, he told himself. He had matched himself against men who lived by their guns many times. But something about this set-up was wrong.

He walked slowly up the hill to the Miners' Bar. He stood under the wooden awning for a time, listening to the multiple voices of the saloon. Johnny Bullis was boasting in a loud, liquor-fortified voice: what he wasn't going to do to this old stage bum, Holbrook, wasn't worth doing. . . .

Grif put out his hand to open the door. Then he let it fall to his side. He was seeing himself telling Annie Benson what he had done. *"I just killed your husband, Annie. Now we can get married."*

Grif heard the blast of Hellfire Galvin's stage horn. He sighed and went back down the street. Buckskin Johnny Bullis had won this round.

Grif had ridden with better company than Hellfire Galvin. Galvin drove like a maniac, hardly looking at the road, keeping the ponies at a dead run except when he stopped to rest them. He sang hymns in a whining voice, punctuated by the popping of his whip.

Banjo Harris's tollgate was open, the stubby stage man standing beside it. Without slowing down, Galvin dug a gold piece from his pocket and flung it at Harris. They swept on.

They cut sharply from the toll road up a narrow trail that led them deep into the woods. They came from the forest onto a plateau overlooking a steep, whispering valley, the bottom of it already in dusk. "Elk River Basin," Hellfire Galvin grunted. "Part of Will Crocker's range."

Part! Grif could see that the main valley was at least ten miles across, that three long arms of it invaded the mountains on the east. Up on a high bench, above the middle of these arms, windows flashed with the ruddy light of the sunset. Crocker's castle, as Jenny Benson had called it, commanded the whole basin.

Hellfire flung the stagecoach down a twisting path that took them to the bottom of the valley. It was dark when they came out onto the flats. With the lamps spraying a flickering wash over the road, they rattled on through a pleasant country of oak and digger pine, with a dozen small streams to feed the grass just coming through the dark earth.

Eastward up the valley they ran. From the middle fork of the valley a ledge-like trail took them up another thousand feet to Crocker's castle.

The bench was a half mile wide, scantily timbered and without water. At the brink of it, Will Crocker's artisans had piled adobe brick upon brick until the result was a ranch house as solid as the mountain itself. The house was low-roofed, with deep-set windows. On the long gallery stood the rancher and a girl, silhouetted by the windows.

Will Crocker stood with one hand on the rail as they went

up the steps. He said: "Who's your friend, Hellfire?"

Galvin looked at Grif and said: "By hokey, I never thought to ask!"

Grif said: "Grif Holbrook." They went inside, Crocker taking the girl's arm. In the light Grif saw that it was Jenny Benson. She was looking mighty pretty in a green and white plaid shirt and a trim riding skirt, with a ribbon to hold back her hair. But Grif wondered what she was doing here.

The interior of the house was of pueblo construction, with a great fireplace at one end of the room. The door was oak, reinforced with strap iron. A long dining table was already set, and Will Crocker said: "You're just in time, boys. Warm yourselves with some *aguardiente* and we'll eat."

Crocker seemed a pleasant sort. He had an informal, California way about him. Standing in front of the fire, he looked long and lean, a man of forty with a lithe, athletic frame. He was no armchair rancher, by the look of him.

Crocker's foreman, a heavy-boned, taciturn man, sat beside Grif. Grif kept glancing at Jenny. There was a tension in the girl; she was not at ease. She seemed frightened.

"Quite a place you've got, Crocker," Grif told his host. "A rabbit couldn't nibble your grass without your knowing it."

Crocker smiled. "You've got to pick your spots in this country. Up here, one man could stand off a thousand." He seemed to know about Grif's business in California, for he added: "How are you coming with the hard-headed Missus Benson . . . all deference to her charming daughter!"

Jenny flushed.

"Not so good," Grif said.

"No," Crocker said, "and you won't. I tried to buy the line, myself, just as an investment, but it's not for sale. But I'm still after it. I'm going to marry into the family and work from the inside!"

He smiled at Jenny's embarrassment, and Grif, watching her closely, wondered if Annie Benson knew where her daughter was tonight. Jenny seemed to read his thoughts.

"Imagine me getting lost in this country," she said to him. "I thought I knew every foot of it. I went up to the sawmill to order some lumber, and I decided to come back a different way. I certainly did! I was lost five hours before I stumbled into the basin!"

"That was my good fortune," said Crocker. "I sent a Mexican over to tell Annie you'll be back tomorrow, Jenny. No sense in trying to ride back tonight."

Grif rolled a cigarette. He said: "I'll tell you what I came for, Crocker. It looks like I might have to build a detour. . . . Logically, it would go right across your range. I'd like to arrive at some kind of a figure with you for the trespass rights."

Crocker was drinking a tawny wine, sipping it with almost sensual enjoyment. He held the glass to the light, peering through the amber liquid. "I don't think I'd be interested, Holbrook," he drawled. "You'd better go around the other side of Lake Tahoe."

Grif said: "That's Galvin's route. It looks to me like a stage road would make your land more valuable."

"Where there's stages rattling through timber land every day," stated Will Crocker, "you're going to have forest fires and every other damned nuisance. I can't afford it. Sorry."

The way he threw down the remainder of the wine put a period to the talk.

After dinner, Hellfire Galvin said: "You want to show me where to leave the hosses, Will?"

The men left the house. Grif was alone with Jenny. Her fears came to her lips in a rush.

"Thank heaven you came, Mister Holbrook! I'll tell you why I came. I was worried about Adam. When he left to hunt his troops today, I followed him. He was heading for the basin, and somehow I'm not quite sure of Will Crocker. I followed him until I found his horse, just over the ridge. I came on to the house . . . but there's no trace of him. I'm afraid to ask, for fear I'll spoil something for him. And yet . . . if Will is involved in the disappearance of the troops. . . ."

Grif said: "Lock your door tonight and put a chair against it. I've got the best nose in the Union for trouble. If he's in a tight, I'll find him."

Grif did not retire until Jenny had gone to her room. Crocker led him through the big, U-shaped building, down ringing corridors to a bedroom opening on an inside patio. He did not undress, but lay on a hard cot with only his boots off. A stone fountain babbled in the patio. Grif recalled the absence of streams on the bench; somewhere there must have been an artesian well to supply the water pressure for a fountain. The tinkle of thin ice, like the music of glass wind chimes, seemed to work away the tension of his taut nerves and muscles, to draw his senses from his tired body into the moonlight-flooded patio. . . .

A hand clutched him solidly by the shoulder. Grif reared up. Adam Stubbs whispered: "Don't wake up fightin', dang it."

Grif blew out his cheeks with relief. "How'd you find me?" he demanded. "What you doing here, anyway?"

"Nosin' around," Stubbs said tersely. "And findin' things! I heard you snoring. After listening to you two nights in a stagecoach, I won't be forgetting your bass notes very quick. Pull on your boots. I'm going to show you something."

Grif followed him down the hall, which was black except for slices of moonlight from under the doors. Stubbs opened the door to the kitchen; the warm air was flavored with the spice of chili. Red coals in the stove gave a flickering light. Stubbs opened a cupboard door. He lit a candle and showed Grif the iron ladder leading down a sort of well. Then he started down quickly, with Grif following.

They descended about twenty-five feet. At the bottom they were in a rough-walled tunnel with a sandy bed. Stubbs lighted a wall lamp. Looking about them, Grif began to realize what Adam Stubbs had stumbled onto.

Stubbs was whispering, although he could have shouted and his voice would hardly have reached the room above them. "I got suspicious when I found a reservoir above the ranch house. What does a cowman want with a reservoir? He's not doing any irrigating. There's plenty of springs down below for his cattle."

"All right," Grif said. "What does he want it for?"

Stubbs gestured. "He dams up the water from a creek where it goes underground, and he's got a ready-made tunnel! The old underground streambed is made to order! Now, who wants a tunnel unless he's in some kind of undercover work? I left my horse up there, found the entrance in some brush, and came down. Did you ever see a sweeter set-up? Look at this!"

Carrying the lantern, he trudged through the sand past a turn, to come out in a small room. A printing press was the central object of interest. There were a half dozen gun racks filled with everything from new Springfields to handmade muzzle-loaders. The tunnel had been walled up here to form a round chamber.

"This is where they print their propaganda," said the major. "It's also an arsenal. Will Crocker may run cattle, Grif, but he's also ramrodding some Bear Flag Rebels."

"Did you find your troops?"

"Not exactly. Just a lot of tracks."

While Stubbs was still speaking, Grif stepped quickly backward two steps, putting himself against the wall. Thus, he was close to the man who slipped around the corner. Grif was in the shadows. The lamp light fell full upon the lean, hungry features of Hellfire Galvin.

Galvin had a sawed-off shotgun in his hands. Death stared Major Adam Stubbs directly in the eye, from the surprise etched on Galvin's features—Grif Holbrook took the risk of it upon himself by throwing a looping blow at the Rebel's head.

Galvin gasped and swung the gun, firing as he moved, so that the charge went between the two men. The explosion was a physical impact against Grif's body. He felt his knuckles take Galvin behind the ear. Galvin went down on his face.

Grif swung up his Colt and waited beside the corner for anyone who might have come with the preacher. The tunnel was soundless except for the whooping of retreating echoes. Grif ventured a glance that proved Galvin had been alone. He went back to inspect the Rebel.

Stubbs had Hellfire's gun. Hellfire had not moved. "You dropped him like a hog in the slaughter pen," Stubbs said. "This is a nice little mess, ain't it?"

Grif scratched his stubbled cheek. "I don't think he saw me. I'll go back and try to bluff it out with Crocker. We ain't ready to move yet, not till we find those troops. If it wasn't for Jenny. . . ."

Adam Stubbs's eyes widened; he looked almost boyish in his surprise. "What about Jenny?" he asked.

"Why, she's upstairs," Grif told him. "She was following you to keep you out of trouble."

Sweat broke out on Stubbs's face. He looked less like a soldier than ever, more like a scared youngster. "My God!" he said. "We've got to get her out, Grif."

Grif squeezed his arm. "You let me worry about Jenny

Benson. I don't look for any trouble with Crocker. If Galvin's able to drive tomorrow, Jenny and I will go back to Harris's with him. Meet us there and we'll go on together in the stage."

IV

Galvin showed up for breakfast. He had circles under his eyes, and his conversation was sparser than ever. Jenny, Grif thought, was a first-rate little actress. She was bright and chatty and terribly grateful to Will Crocker for putting her up. She exclaimed over the cook's *huevos rancheros*. She appeared genuinely sorry when it came time to leave.

Crocker stood smiling at the foot of the steps as they rolled off. But between them, Grif knew, a change had come which had cocked a gun. There was distrust in Will Crocker's heart; no amount of smiling could hide that from Grif's shrewd eyes.

Hellfire Galvin left them at the Rimrock station. Banjo Harris hitched up his team, and they started for Annie Benson's. Grif rode the box with him.

They had gone only a mile when they encountered Stubbs, sitting his pony beside the road. The stage driver let him tie his horse on behind with Jenny's.

"Feller must be mighty sweet on a gal," Harris told Grif, "when he'll pay eight bucks to set with her!" He gave Grif sharp sidelong glances as they rode. "Bet a pretty you ran into trouble with Crocker over your detour!" he said sagely.

It was damned annoying how things got around in this country, Grif thought. How did Harris know why he had gone up there? He said casually: "Not what I'd call trouble. Crocker seems glad to know he's going to have a stage line within a mile of his ranch house."

Harris looked shocked, his small, piggish eyes blank. "You mean," he said, "you really aim to build a detour? Why, that'd cost you a fortune!"

"Not that buying up your line and the widder Benson's wouldn't," Grif grunted.

For a while Banjo Harris was silent. He was feeling the ropes against his back, and he was not liking them. He said: "If it looks like you can't meet my price, Holbrook, I might . . . well, a feller can always dicker. I might not . . ."—he essayed a grin—"might not be too hard."

Grif grunted. In the next instant he was yelling and pointing and grabbing for his gun all in one pinwheel of motion. "Guerrillas! Whip them nags up! We'll have to run for it!"

Out of the manzanita thickets flanking the road plunged a dozen horsemen. Grif saw something he had not seen since Army days: flashing sabers—sabers that two of the attackers were swinging to put the lead ponies out of action. Most of the other men carried carbines. All of them wore dark-gray short-coats, in an attempt at uniformity, but other than this, clothing, harness, and men were a random catch.

Banjo Harris was a statue of terror. He sat straight as a stick on the seat, letting the horses run. It was Grif Holbrook's old half-breed Colt that lined out on the man charging the off leader. It was his shoulder that took the buck of the .44, his ball that went through the man's neck and rolled him from the saddle.

John Butterfield liked to say that there was nothing pretty about Grif but the way he could shoot from the deck of a Concord. He worked best when the action was hottest. Grif pressed his unshaven cheek against the stock and brought the next man under his sights. Guns were cracking back in the dust. Grif fired again, and the other guerrilla clutched his shoulder and dropped away.

Grif scrambled over the seat. He gained the deck and lay on his belly between the railings, firing into the mass of riders. He saw a horse break its run and go down.

A gun spoke inside the coach. Major Adam Stubbs was getting some of the action he had loved, back with the Sixth. But what about Jenny? The only pulse of fear in Grif was for her.

Harris was keeping that twenty-foot gap between the guerrillas and the stage. While it held, they had some chance to break away. Grif could throw a lot straighter shot from his position than could the riders. Lead was splintering the body of the Concord, but a lucky shot was all he worried about.

Before long the lucky shot came by—a hot, tearing pain gouged Grif's back. Just for a moment he was sinking into a brilliant well of pain. Then the pain itself dragged him back to consciousness. He fired again until the gun was empty; he slipped a fresh cylinder into the breech.

The riders were closer; they were too damned close. Some of their shots were ripping splinters from the deck. Grif turned his head.

"Give them ponies the whip!" he yelled. Then he saw how Banjo Harris was leaning out over the dashboard, the ribbons pulling slowly through his lax hand. He saw Harris suddenly crumple and drop between the wheelers. Grif was just able to recover the lines before Harris went.

What he didn't know about stage driving was plenty, but the principles of making any horse move faster were the same. He put business into the pop of the whip. The ponies began to run.

Cold Springs station couldn't be far ahead. That, Grif knew, was not good, either. No use turning a chase into a siege at Annie Benson's place.

Just when the guerrillas dropped away, he did not know. Gradually he realized the hoof sounds in their wake had died. Stubbs's gun no longer barked. Grif looked back. The road through the forest was clear.

He did some somber thinking on the way in. Will Crocker, if he had arranged this party, had exhibited shrewdness typical of him. Why kill a man in your front yard when you could send the dogs out to do it ten miles away? He would send out the dogs with sharper teeth, next time, although the rake of one fang throbbed steadily in Grif's back.

So now they knew, at least, what they were up against. Not just a couple of money-hungry stage line proprietors, but men with a doctrine to spread. You could usually bluff a man out if money was all he had to gain. Crusaders, no matter what they were fighting for, sank in their teeth and held on. Maybe California, heavy with gold and cattle and wheat, would make the men who severed it from the Union the richest men in the world.

Grif Holbrook was disgusted. Damn Ben Holladay! If it weren't for him, he'd be on his way south right now. Damn Buckskin Johnny Bullis, who stood like a brick wall between Grif and the only woman he had ever loved.

Annie Benson, standing in the yard, saw Grif up there on the box. She must have known instantly that things were not right. She saw the bullet holes in the stage, and Grif saw her cheeks lose color. Adam Stubbs's hand helped Jenny down. Annie clasped the girl in her arms, and they were both crying.

Grif went inside. There was stew in a Dutch oven over the fire. He helped himself. Annie came inside. He heard her gasp.

"Why, Grif! You're hurt!"

She made him take off his coat and shirt and peel his new woolen underwear, already ruined, down to the waist. He lay

91

on a cot while she cleaned the long gash in his back, making tender, clucking sounds as she worked. Annie fixed a bandage for him, and Grif put on a clean shirt and let Jenny take his coat to try to clean it.

Grif said: "Annie, there's a lot of places I'd rather see you than here. This country's going to catch fire. I wish I could make you sell."

For the moment they were alone in the room. Annie Benson's eyes were sober. "I'm going to tell you something I've never told anyone else," she said. "I haven't sold before because I'm afraid. I'm afraid to stay and afraid to sell. I'm a lone, 'lorn woman, Grif. I know nothing about business. I've seen what has happened to other widow women who tried to run a business. Too often some man has taken it over, for next to nothing. I've been afraid that would happen to me if I got into a deal with a big outfit like the Great Overland. And I've got Jenny to take care of for a while longer."

A log moved in the fireplace. Annie watched the sparks fly up the chimney. She said: "I've been thinking I would sell out, after all, Grif."

Grif said: "I promise you'll get all it's worth. We can handle it through banker Fergus, if you like."

Annie said: "No. I'd want cash, and as soon as possible."

Grif was disturbed. Everything was ironing out—Banjo Harris was out of the picture, rest his soul, and now Annie was ready to sell—but something bothered him. "I've only got fifteen thousand to draw on," he told her. "That was supposed to be earnest money for both lines. I could get the rest in a month."

"Fifteen thousand would be all right," Annie said. "But I'd want it tomorrow."

In the moment's hush Grif heard the strike of horseshoes in the yard. He looked at Annie; he saw in her face a hundred little fears. He saw how her fingers knit and unknit themselves. "Annie," he said, "has Johnny Bullis been here?"

Annie Benson sank back in the chair. "He came up this morning. He said he's staying. He rode out to hunt. That's him coming back." She added dully: "I thought maybe I could take Jenny and get away."

The door opened, causing the flames to crowd up the flue and then, as it slammed, to subside. Buckskin Johnny Bullis, striking his cold hands together, grinned at them from the door.

Bullis leaned his carbine against the wall, by the door. He gave Grif a look of sardonic amusement. "I reckon I won't need this," he said. "I decided to stay around a while longer, Holbrook."

Grif's fingers bunched until the knuckles ached. He said: "Say the word, Annie, and I'll pitch him out."

Annie stood up. "I think you'd better stay in town, Grif," she said. "Apparently you can't both stay here without fighting. And I have enough trouble without that."

Bullis went over to the stew kettle and dipped out a chunk of beef with his fingers. "Don't throw him out on my account," he said to Annie. "I came back for a chance of grub and some blankets. That buck got away from me up on Strawberry Peak. Damned if I won't run him down before I quit. I ain't ate venison since I left Arizona."

Grif was noticing something, that Bullis wore nothing but a pony-skin vest over his shirt, although it was cold outside. It was a small fact, but his mind began to mull it over.

Bullis's black eyes met his. "I'm what you might call a man of leisure now," he stated. "Me and Annie thought we'd sell out and do some travelin'. That's what you wanted, ain't it . . . to buy the outfit from us?"

Grif ground his teeth together. Annie was watching him

from the door to her bedroom. All his impulses commanded him to take Bullis by the ears and give him a first-class knuckle currying. But there was a time and place for such things. He slammed out of the cabin.

He sat on a stump near the trees and smoked, trying to sort his thoughts. Pretty soon he saw Bullis come out the back door with a couple of blankets over his shoulder, and a sack of food. He went to the corral and left these things by the gate while he caught a pack animal. He slipped a hackamore over the horse's head and left it tied, going into the harness shed then for a pack saddle.

Maybe it was the cocky swing of his shoulders that went across Grif's nerves like a file; maybe it was the way he let a cigarette hang from his lip as though it were pasted there. Whatever it was, a raw, compelling hatred sent Grif Holbrook toward the harness shed.

Bullis, back in the shadows, started when Grif entered. He was pulling a pair of kaks off a rack. He let them drop and faced the other. If he had any ideas about a gun fight, he discarded them when he saw that Grif's Colt was already trained on his belly.

"Unbuckle your gun, Johnny," Grif said. "Drop it and kick it over here."

"You ain't much on guts, are you?" Bullis remarked. But his gun thumped on the dirt floor.

Grif said: "I decided to make good on what I told you before. You want to get on that horse right now and ride? Or do I have to persuade you?"

Bullis began to get the drift. His black eyes sparkled. "If it's fists," he said, "I'd shore like to be persuaded."

"It's fists," said Grif. "I couldn't ever get the satisfaction out of putting a slug in you that I will out of taking you apart limb by limb." He left his gun and Bullis's outside the door.

He took off his coat with something like eagerness. They moved together in the middle of the floor.

"I don't know what it is about your face that makes me want to change it," Grif growled. "But I sure aim to make some alterations."

Bullis came at him. He fought as he lived, recklessly. Grif blocked the fists that slashed at his head and let the others drum against his midriff. Behind the gunman's punches was a jolting power. Bullis's rush tailed off, while a frown of doubt colored his face. Grif Holbrook stood under his attack like a boulder in a flood. And Grif was shooting out his own right, now. It caught Bullis in the face. It split his upper lip and let a cascade of blood out; it sent him to his knees.

Grif waited for him. In his impatience he kept making and unmaking his fists. Buckskin Johnny Bullis shook off the stupor. He came back, swearing. Grif rocked him with a blow over the heart; Bullis grunted, badly hurt. Right then, he changed his direction of attack. He put the haymakers back in the bag; he took out a weapon called craft. You couldn't whip this old shotgun messenger by crowding him, but maybe you could wear him down. Forty-five generally gave out quicker than thirty-five.

Grif could see the decision-making in his eyes. He thought: *I've got the answer to that one, too, Johnny.*

Bullis kept backing, ducking, jabbing. Grif followed him around the room, swinging like a fool, spending himself. The gunman backed into a sawhorse and sprawled, but Grif waited while he scrambled up.

Grif was breathing hard, his chest laboring. It did not escape the other man. He decided the moment had come. He fired a blow at Grif's chin and came in right behind it.

Somehow Grif's chin wasn't there. His head tilted, letting the fist slip past so that Johnny Bullis was thrown off balance.

Grif cocked his fist and went to work. . . .

He went outside, into the clear, cold sunlight. He felt spiritually exalted, as though he had shown a sinner the true path.

He heard a file rasp in the shed and, walking that way, found Adam Stubbs fitting a new shoe to the horse Annie had loaned him. Jenny sat on a bale of hay, watching him. Bullis's horse was tethered nearby, and that was what Grif wanted to see. He stopped beside it and inspected the roll behind the cantle, and then he went into the shed.

"Figuring on a ride?" Grif asked Stubbs quietly.

"I'm going back and trail those buckaroos that killed Harris."

Jenny's brow was puckered with concern. "You'll never get away a second time, Adam," she said. "What can one man do against a hundred and fifty?"

When the major only grunted, Grif said: "Stick around a while, sonny. I figure somebody's going to lead us to 'em if we wait long enough." He added, nodding at Bullis's pony: "Look yonder."

At first Stubbs's expression showed that he saw only the pinto, still saddled and standing placidly. There was dried sweat on its hide, evidence of its having run. When he saw what was tied behind the cantle, he dropped his file. "Bullis! So he was in that pack!"

The object on the saddle was one of the dark-gray short-coats that the guerrillas had worn, rolled and tied by the saddle strings. There was no mistaking the color. It explained why the gunman had come in from a deer hunt in summer clothing.

"He's going out to track down a buck," Grif told the major. "Maybe we'll just swing along behind and help bring the carcass back. Trust a cut-back like him to be mixed up in a revolution."

Some time during the afternoon, Buckskin Johnny Bullis stumbled to the horse trough and washed up. Grif kept out of his way, not wanting a gunfight. Evidently the gunman had taken Grif's advice seriously this time. A couple of hours before sundown he pulled out.

Almost immediately, Annie came from her bedroom. She was wearing a brown woolen dress and a bonnet that tied under the chin. She laid a paper on the table before Grif, where he was drinking warmed-over coffee.

"You said you'd give me fifteen thousand dollars cash for the Mountain Express Line," she said. "There is the deed. Will you give me a check?"

Grif took her hands. "What are you going to do, Annie?"

Annie's lower lip trembled. "I'm having Sam take us to Placerville to get the money. I'll buy some things we have to have and then come back. We'll stay here until the next east-bound stage comes through."

Sharp fingers were tearing at Grif's heart. This was how it should be, but for him it was not going to be easy. He glanced at the document, slowly folded it, and put it in his pocket. "I reckon it's best," he said. "If I don't see you again, Annie, why . . . why, good luck."

"You've been awfully good to me, Grif," Annie said. She smiled, a little tearfully; she bent, and her lips brushed his cheek. Jenny came into the room, looking like a girlish replica of her mother. Grif walked outside with them.

He watched the spring wagon rattle away. Then he went inside and blew his nose and recalled what someone had said about old fools.

V

They gave Buckskin Johnny Bullis a half hour, so that their following would not be obvious. Then they rode after him, with their rifles across their pommels.

For a while the sign followed a plainly marked trail that cut south across the meadow. Later, it branched, making trailing difficult in the mats of pine needles. They crossed a couple of ridges. From the crest of the second they looked down into a scimitar-shaped cañon curving away to the southwest.

It was gloomy and cold at the bottom. Frost-needled air packed down upon them. High above, the last rays of the sun reddened the trees. They could no longer read Bullis's trail, but they rode slowly on, hoping to catch sight of his campfire in the deep, silent woods.

As complete darkness flooded the cañon, Grif growled: "I say we make camp. Night riding in this country is too risky."

"According to my map," said Stubbs, "the cañon opens out into a park a little ways ahead. That would be a logical place for a camp. Let's ride another fifteen minutes."

Before they had gone five, they knew his hunch was right. In the breeze blowing gently up the cañon they tasted the odors of pinewood smoke and coffee. They left their horses, silenced their spurs, and went ahead on foot.

Now the narrow cañon fanned out into a park, the shape and size of which the night made secret. But the darkness only intensified the brilliance of a string of campfires blazing along the bank of a stream. They could make out, beyond, ordered blocks of tents.

As they watched, one of the fires seemed to black out. Then it came back, while the one next to it went out. Grif made out the form of a sentry walking his post only a few rods ahead of them, between them and the fires. With the pressure of his hand, he cautioned Adam Stubbs to silence.

The sentry was going away from him. Grif went ahead, timing his footfalls with those of the guard. The man paced wearily, his rifle canted carelessly across his shoulder, in the fashion of a sentry whose relief is overdue.

Grif said: "Guard!"

The sentry started, turning quickly. Grif's fist was already moving. He took the man on the point of the chin. He caught him as he sagged, lowering him noiselessly to the grass. Stubbs came up on a trot.

Grif pulled the short-coat off the unconscious man. He gave it to the major. "Put this on," he said. "Them yellow cavalry slashes stand out like coach lamps."

Around the fires men were eating. Stubbs's eyes shone as he regarded the soldiers of his "command"—Rebels, now. Could anything be done with them, or had the doctrine Hellfire Galvin preached been fused into the very bones of them?

They skirted the left end of the camp, making their way to the tent at the head of the company street. According to the usual arrangement, the commanding officer's quarters would be located at this point. They saw that the interior of the tent was illuminated by a lantern. They went to their bellies in the grass and crawled to the back of it, hearing the voices within.

Johnny Bullis said: "It's strictly business with me, Galvin. If the profit ain't in it, I don't play the game."

Hellfire Galvin's voice had a raw edge. "Crocker will give you a note for twice what that jerk-line outfit will bring anywhere else. The point is, if it's sold to Ben Holladay, we can expect no end of trouble. As it is, Annie Benson can't raise too much fuss. She's a small operator. We can expect trouble, sooner or later, but we aren't prepared for it yet."

"I don't care about that," said Bullis. "I'm talking about cash. When I agreed to help Crocker, I didn't mean I would do it for exercise. How much will Crocker pay me for the stage line, and when?"

"Fifty thousand," Galvin said succinctly. "Payable within six months. We've had expenses. Forty thousand dollars to equip this outfit! Three thousand in salaries every month." He added, his voice warming: "If you'd be willing to work right with us, you'd get ten times fifty thousand. This is big, Bullis! One of these days we'll strike. Bear Flag outfits from here to San Diego will rise to sever all communication with the Union. Then, my boy, the ones who are behind the movement will have power you've never dreamed of!"

"Maybe," Bullis said skeptically. "Me, I'll take my money in good U.S. gold. I'll sell to Crocker for thirty thousand . . . cash."

Grif could visualize the resentment in Galvin's lean countenance. "You do a lot of bragging," Galvin was saying, "for somebody that muffed a job like you did today." He said with some satisfaction: "Look at you! He not only broke up that stage ruckus but fist-whipped you into the bargain."

"Next time it will be different," Bullis said slowly. "You can keep your damned would-be dragoons. I'll do the job myself . . . in my own way."

Galvin said: "You've got two days to take care of them. A thousand apiece."

Adam Stubbs put his lips close to Grif's ear. "Hold them for me," he said. "I'm going out and give the boys the old recruiting pitch."

He went crawling away. Grif wagged his head. Stubbs was a wild-eyed fool when it came to strategy. What could he offer his derelict troops but court-martial if they came back to the fold?

There was a slit door in the back, in front of which Grif crouched. Suddenly, sharply, Adam Stubbs's voice rang through the camp: *"Fall in!"*

Grif plowed through the slit, landing on his belly to look up at the two startled Rebels. Galvin sat on a log, his shirt off, preparing for bed. Buckskin Johnny Bullis squatted on his heels, his fingers fashioning a cigarette.

"Keep your mouths shut," Grif directed. "Adam Stubbs is going to say a few words to the boys. We're going to wait right here and listen."

Men were running from the fires; men were piling out of their tents, pulling on clothes as they came. Through the open flap, Grif could see the major standing near a fire. Stubbs's voice was brassy with authority. "Sergeants . . . dress up those lines!"

Hellfire Galvin's stark, bearded features were purpling. Grif turned the muzzle of the gun to cover him. "Not a bleat out of you, you sanctimonious old sinner."

Stubbs barked again: "Report!" Up and down the lines non-commissioned officers parroted: "All present or accounted for, sir!"

Up to this point the troopers had not known but that he was one of their own men. He had an aggressive, forty-lashes sort of authority in his manner; when he gave a command, it came back off the cañon so loud that the men jumped.

While they stood at attention, the major began to talk. He told them who he was. He told them what the Army did to men who deserted while their brothers were dying in action. He said: "The only thing between you and a firing squad is the fact that you're green recruits. The Army doesn't punish men who disobey through ignorance." A lieutenant, the adjutant, faced him woodenly a few yards away. "Have these men ever had the Articles of War read to them?" Stubbs demanded.

"No, sir."

Major Stubbs took a small volume out of his pocket and began to sketch through the Articles of War. The troops were silent, dazed. Finishing, Stubbs said: "From here on out you're responsible for your actions as soldiers. You have taken oath to defend your country. If you continue as Rebels, you will be hunted down to the last man . . . I assume that the man who took you from Cold Springs represented himself as a regular. Later, I suppose, he sold you on the idea that you could do yourselves more good by fighting to separate California from the Union."

Bullis and Galvin were suffering silent apoplexy. Grif lay there and enjoyed it; he was even beginning to believe that Adam Stubbs might swing it, although the only weapon he had against one hundred and fifty deserters' rifles was his tongue.

Stubbs was saying: "You've enlisted in a fool's crusade. You joined originally to help make all men free. How do you know what your bosses have in mind for you? Maybe you won't have much better than slavery yourselves, after they confiscate everything they want. If you stay with Lincoln, you know what you have. I promise there will be no punishment for any of you. I ask for a vote by roll call. If you're ready to change colors, answer . . . 'Yes'."

The voices were not all strong. Some came resentfully, some timorously. Most of them were uncertain. But they were all "Yes" voices. Major Stubbs had taken them by sheer force of surprise. "Your commander is already in custody in his tent," he told them. "Starting tomorrow, you will drill under me. You won't find it easy. But you'll be the fittest soldiers west of the Mississippi."

He came back to the tent with the lieutenant and a detail of men to guard Hellfire Galvin and Buckskin Johnny Bullis. Grif Holbrook was not yet able to accept it; it had all been too easy. Beside the officers' campfire, Stubbs drank thirstily from Grif's canteen.

"They'll soldier for me," he said with tight satisfaction. "And, by God, I think they'll like it!"

But there were a few who would not soldier. They had voted "Yes" because they had no choice, with the majority against them. That was how Grif figured it out when, toward dawn, the sergeant of the guard awakened them.

The man was excited. "They got away, Major. Some of the men laid out the guards and helped them escape."

Stubbs was pulling on his boots. "When did it happen?"

"Right after the third relief went on, sir. We didn't find out till the others went out to relieve them."

Stubbs said: "Have the men assemble and we'll find out how many got away."

The roll call showed forty-five men missing. The loyal troopers still numbered nearly a hundred. Stubbs gave the order for a hasty breakfast. He and Grif led the column out in pursuit, just as dawn was pouring its ruddy colors down the cañon sides.

By the appearance of the hoof marks, Hellfire Galvin ran his dragoons with the same fiery recklessness he showed on the box of a Concord. As soon as the Rebels had cleared camp, the horses had been put to a lope. Only in the steepest pitches were the horses walked.

"Let 'em run," Grif said. "We'll catch 'em all the sooner when the ponies play out. Where they're going, they'll go fast, but it ain't going to be far."

He began to grow apprehensive when he realized they were retracing exactly the course by which Bullis had come to the camp. Grif thanked God Annie and Jenny had gone to Placerville for the night. Bullis was a cold-blooded, vengeful man.

They came to a place where the force they were following

had split. One party cut due west over the hills, toward Elk River Basin, where Will Crocker had his castle. The others apparently were heading for Annie Benson's.

There was a heavy ball of apprehension on Grif's stomach. He met Stubbs's eyes and knew the same fear was in him—what if the women had come back last night?

Grif pulled a half dollar out of his pocket. He said—"Call it."—and flipped the coin in the air.

"Tails," said Stubbs. It was tails that gleamed up at them from the ground where the coin fell.

Stubbs swung out of line and raised his arm. "Right-hand file . . . column right, *ho!*"

Adam Stubbs took his detail at a jog toward Cold Springs station. Grif Holbrook swore darkly and led his men along the other fork. He told himself that Annie was all right. She had likely not even started from Placerville. All Bullis could do was to burn the station. But he was surly and nervous as they rode. It was plain now that the Rebels were making for the safety of Crocker's castle. He wondered how Will Crocker would welcome such guests. Crocker was the kind who liked to let somebody else take his risks.

About nine o'clock they came to the northern rim of Elk River Basin. Far below them a party of horsemen was making dust. Without glasses, Grif could only estimate the number. Twenty-five or thirty was his guess. Probably the raiding party under Bullis, whose trail Stubbs had taken; the trail he himself was following would strike the valley farther east. So the whole force would be in the big adobe fortress to receive them.

Grif was recalling the boast Will Crocker had made: *one man could stand off a thousand!*

They worked down the narrow goat path to the floor of the valley. Long before they cut up the wedge-like cañon that led

104

to Crocker's, the Rebels had gone clattering up the switch-back path that climbed the last mile to the ranch house.

Grif dismounted his men, left the horses with guards, and took the detail through sparse stands of digger pine dotting the wide floor of the cañon. This kind of work was not new to him. He knew what it could cost to go charging wild-eyed up to the fortress: that lesson he had learned at Monterrey, in '46, where Mexican guns almost blew to pieces his platoon, under a certain Lieutenant U.S. Grant.

In his mind he sketched the terrain—the blockhouse-like building almost at the edge of the cliff, behind and around it the treeless expanse of benchland. No chance for a charge from the rear. Not much chance on the trail, either. The trail switchbacked up the south wall of the cañon, in full view of snipers in the ranch house. Night offered the only possible chance for an attack without terrific losses. A siege might last for weeks.

A ball whined off the ground in the midst of the men. Grif ignored it. More shots fell among them, but he kept the detail at a measured pace up the cañon. At a quarter of a mile, a hit on a moving target would be luck, and these men needed the tempering of moving ahead under fire.

But Grif Holbrook was thinking about Annie. What the hell was keeping Stubbs? He should have been in the basin, by now.

Then, in the distance, a rifle flung tumbling echoes across the valley. Stubbs was bringing his men into the basin.

VI

At the foot of the trail, Grif dispersed his men and waited. A half hour later Stubbs brought his platoon through the brush. Grif did not have to ask him what he knew; Stubbs's face told him that. The major was grinning broadly.

"Grif," he said, "she loves me!"

Grif scowled. He said: "Where'd you find them?"

"Man," Stubbs said, "I was sick! The station was burned. We were poking through the ashes when they came along. They'd left early. An hour before and Bullis's gang would have jumped them! They were going to take the afternoon stage to Denver, but I talked them out of it."

"How do you know Jenny loves you?" Grif demanded. Jealousy was gnawing at his vitals; Stubbs could grin—he didn't have a second-hand husband in his way.

Stubbs's color heightened. "She told me. If . . . when I come back, we'll go to Placerville and find a preacher."

Lead picked with dry fingers through the bush. "You can find a preacher a lot closer than Placerville," Grif declared. "There's one in Crocker's castle that'll be saying eulogies over us tonight if we don't outsmart him. You've been to the Point, Stubbs. Did they teach you how to take places that can't be took?"

Responsibility settled on Stubbs's shoulders. "Artillery would do it," he said. "But all I've got is ball and bayonet. We might try a charge. After dark."

"You'd lose half the men as they came over the bench. The doors are oak and iron. They'd raise hell with us before we broke in . . . if we did."

Stubbs looked at the men crouching near them in the manzanita thickets. Without uniforms, there was nothing military about them. The deficiency went deeper than that. The troops were completely untried. Some would undoubtedly break when the air droned with death and screams rose over the roar of musketry. A charge that veteran troopers might carry off would bring these recruits to their knees.

Stubbs said: "I could send them up the cliff and avoid the trail. But they'd still be clay pigeons when they rushed the house. There's that tunnel under the house. . . ." He shook his head. "Crocker will put ten men down there, if he's got a brain in his head. We'd never get through."

Grif thoughtfully worked the hammer of his carbine. "Stubbs," he said suddenly, "if you take your men up the cliff, I can flush them out for you! Give me a squad. That's all I'll need."

He made a diagram in the dirt with his finger. It was all so pat that Stubbs swore softly at his own failure to see it. "I ought to be busted to a buck-eared private! Take two squads. We'll get 'em coming and going."

There were still five hours of daylight, but it was a three-hour hike back to the horses and then around the northern rim of the basin. There was at least an hour's work when they reached the entrance of the tunnel that led under Will Crocker's castle. It would be a sundown fight.

Where Granite Creek meandered through the forest, Will Crocker had constructed an earthen dam about one hundred feet long. A flume carried the overflow to a sawmill a mile or two south. Grif poked around the brush until he found the mouth of the tunnel. In a cairn of rocks the stream had sunk through the sand to find its underground channel. Here, Crocker's workmen had shored up the sandy adit with timbers and screened it with clumps of buck brush.

Grif put one squad of dragoons to clearing away the brush, while he looked over the dam to see what was to be done. He counted on the water doing most of the work, but it needed a start.

Six of the men had entrenching tools tied behind their cantles. In relays, the fourteen men went to work gouging a deep notch in the earthwork. Grif walked to the edge of the timber and surveyed the terrain below.

The ranch house was patterned in the shape of a U. On the roof, Grif could see men bellied up to embrasures in the battlements. Every window was grilled with iron. Every door was as stout as cement. He was doing this job the only way it could be done—from the inside.

An hour passed and the notch in the dam was still above water level. Grif bent his broad back to the job. He set a pace that wore out two reliefs of younger men. The sun was only a few minutes above the hills. Grif did not want to make the fight in darkness.

He felt a moistness around his feet and, looking down, realized the water was beginning to pour over the dam into its old channel. A few more shovels full were taken out, then they ran aside to let the water do the job.

It went slowly, turgidly, at first. It gained force; it boiled over the soft clods and rolled them out of the way. It broke through the barricade with a low roar that was like rejoicing. And when it hit the sand, it was traveling fast.

Grif rested on his hunkers. He visualized what would happen when the water reached the barricade Crocker had erected under his fortress, to wall up his arsenal and probably keep anyone from coming at him from downstream. Water would go up that staircase like an artesian well! It would fill the rooms and squirt out the windows. It would dissolve those adobe bricks like so many porous sugar lumps. And Hellfire Galvin and Will Crocker would come running out into a wall of screaming lead. Yes, and Johnny Bullis. You couldn't say it was unethical of Grif if somebody else killed him. But it would make Annie a red-headed widder, just the same.

Grif Holbrook took his men down to the edge of the woods. Two hundred yards of bare ground stretched between them and the house. Grif gave them some hard-bitten advice: "This ain't Gaines Mill, boys. Forget your sabers. Go in with pistols. When they're empty, use your carbines. Then swing 'em like clubs."

He saw the greenish pallor on the faces of some of them. "Strong medicine for your bellies?" he said. "Hell, they're only rabbits we've drove into a pen, and now we're going to stomp them out. Only these rabbits will stomp you, if you give them a chance." He growled: "Hit leather . . . or whatever they say in the cavalry!"

There were signs of disorder in the ranch house. Water was oozing out the cracks; it was dribbling from under the doors. Suddenly a door pulled out of its water-soaked mud jamb and leaned drunkenly outward. A brown flood gushed from the house.

One of the wings went out of perspective. It wasn't wearing its roof quite in plumb. Slowly it was settling by the port. With soft crumbling sounds the outer wall went down.

Grif said: "Let's go!"

The men on the roof were jumping down. Grif split his force, sending them right and left about the house. A Rebel sprawled from a door, saw him, and threw a rifle to his shoulder. Grif's teeth showed as he fired at the upturned face. He swerved around the falling figure to lope over and down the side of the house.

Guns were banging lustily in front. That was where the excitement was, and it was where Grif wanted to be. He saw Adam Stubbs charging the house at a run, his men yelling behind him, bayonets flashing. He saw Will Crocker coming down the steps with a Colt in each hand. There was nothing debonair about Crocker this time. He was a man fighting for his life, fighting with a snarl on his lips. Grif saw his guns tilt toward him. Crocker fired. He missed, because fear had blurred his sights. Grif's shot was true.

Grif left the saddle. Stubbs was yelling at his men, swinging them around to outflank the men escaping. A lot of them were pasty-faced, shaking with fear, but they kept advancing.

Buckskin Johnny Bullis came from the house. Bullis had a cigarette in his lips. He held his gun carelessly, completely in command of himself as he evaluated his chances. Bullis was no coward. He intended to fight, and he was going to make his shots count.

Grif reached Adam Stubbs's side. "Bullis!" he yelled. "Knock him over! He . . . he's out of season, for me."

Stubbs looked at him queerly. His eyes said: *buck fever*. But when he raised his Colt, it was Bullis he hung on his sights.

Grif saw Bullis stagger. He saw him clutch at the porch railing. The gunman raised his gun and found Grif's face in the jumble of moving targets. The Colt jumped in his hand, and Grif's side hurt as though a horse had kicked him.

Again Stubbs fired. Bullis see-sawed over the rail and lay twisted.

Grif felt himself soaring. Pain and exhilaration were making a draft too strong for him.

He could not remember, afterward, how the fight went after that. Stubbs told him that he had gone into the house when Hellfire Galvin did not appear. That he had come out with his old Dragoon pistol smoking, but without Galvin. After that he had collapsed.

It seemed that all he had been doing for a week was getting knocked over in scrapes, while Stubbs walked through them unhurt. The last shots had hardly ceased to echo when he came to. There wasn't much blood in evidence, but an ex-vet, who was serving as company surgeon, told him he had a broken rib.

"No riding for a while," he told Grif.

Grif said: "The hell with that!" He found Stubbs detailing men to various jobs—cooking, wood-gathering, guarding prisoners. "Have somebody saddle my hoss," he told the major.

Stubbs grinned. "You ain't going anywhere, pardner. I'll take your regards to Annie Benson in the morning. She and Jenny were going back to Banjo Harris's place."

"The point is," Grif said, "I'm going right now. I've got worries, son. You've got clear sailing. If somebody will saddle my horse, I'll make it."

Stubbs shook his head as Grif rode away. The rib wasn't making the ride any easier, but the pain was less galling than the uncertainty.

There was still a light in Harris's stage station. Sam Doniphan, the beetle-browed hostler, came from the barn with a Colt in his hand as Grif dismounted before the station. He said: "Name yourself, mister." Doniphan was breathless, juggling with the Colt nervously. There had been too much excitement lately for a man whose life was dedicated to feeding and cleaning up after horses.

Grif said: "Relax, Sam. It's me. Where's the Bensons?"

"Jenny's inside," Doniphan said. "You can knock. Don't know as she'll let you in."

In Grif's stomach there was a sensation of having been kicked. "Where," he asked, "is Annie?"

"Reckoned you knew. Annie took the afternoon stage. Gone east, she didn't say where. Oh, yes!" he said. "Thar was this letter."

He found it in one of his pockets, crumpled and smudged, but still fragrant of lavender sachet. Grif held it in the light falling through the window. The writing was small and neat; the import of it was big enough to shake him.

Grif:

You've done so much for me I can't ever thank you. I don't know how it will come out about Johnny, but I can't afford to wait and see. Jenny is waiting for Adam.

But for now there is too much in the way for us: there's Johnny, and there's still the war to win. Ben Holladay needs you. And yet, I hope you will remember, and wait for,

Your own Annie

Sam, the hostler, squinted at him. He said: "Hey, now! What's the trouble?"

Grif blew his nose. There was concern in Doniphan's simple face. But there was no use trying to explain. He said: "Sam, didn't you ever have a hoss you loved, and then it died or somebody else stole it?"

Doniphan's eyes softened. "Shore!" he said. "I had a rosewood bay gelding oncet. Gawd, if he wasn't a beauty! Why, I could lay down and he'd pick me up by the belt and carry me clean across the yard! Then he got the swinny."

Grif went back in the barn with him and made himself a bed in the hay. He heard all about the last hours of Sam Doniphan's rosewood bay.

"What about this hoss of yours, Grif?" Sam asked.

Grif was lying on his back, staring up into the darkness. "She was a little sorrel mare," he said. "The best little mare I ever did see. One day she just up and took off. But, Sam," he said, "she's got my brand on her. And, by golly, I'll bet dollars to horseshoes she winds up in my pasture yet!"

U.P. Trail Breaker

I

Grif Holbrook was drunk—drunker than he had ever been. A deep loneliness filled him. It was hard to die young, he reflected, but far worse to outlive your time. And Grif's time had ended two years ago, when they had started forging a steel cable to tie California to the Union. In a year or so the Union Pacific would be completed, and the men who had gloriously followed the perilous trade of staging would go into the scrap heap, an odd reward for heroes. Grif Holbrook figured he had an advantage over the rest of the boys in that he had started the long slide a year or so early.

What the hell was he doing in a railroad town, he wondered. Maybe it was the morbid fascination of watching the track gangs at their work and play. Lately, incidentally, it had been all play. Track had not been laid in three weeks. Workers, most of them out of uniform only two years, were loudly decrying the lay-off, and promoters were gloomily biting their nails. Winter was upon them, and there was still a sixty-mile stretch of mountain to cross. It was generally a pretty gloomy time.

Only the camp followers were happy. They weren't all women, either. When men settle down to serious playing, they need saloonkeepers, gamblers, and all the rest of it. The construction camp had been stalled here so long it had even acquired a title: Cheyenne, Wyoming Territory. A few wooden structures stood out conspicuously among the canvas tents. After the camps moved on, a little kernel of civilization might remain here, beside the headboards of those who had lived not wisely, but too well.

At ten o'clock Grif saw Sam Grummond come in. Not all the parasites here purveyed liquor or love. Grummond was working a queer game that Grif hadn't quite figured out. Every night he went through the same routine.

Grif watched him hang his map from the back-bar. The sticky pine bar was suddenly swarming, because the liquor was always free when Sam Grummond dropped in.

"Here you are, gents!" he was saying. He struck the map with his cane. "The little town of Antelope, all ready to burst into life! And tonight I've got news. I'm taking out the first detachment of settlers tomorrow morning, so all you men who've bought lots on Main Street be ready to leave. I furnish the wagons. Anybody else wants to buy before the rush, the land is still going at five dollars a foot."

Grif stood at the end of the bar, where he could study the promoter's face. Men's faces told things their mouths never did. Grummond's was rutted with dissipation. The mouth was crabbed, the eyes cynical, suspicious. But Grummond seemed to have plenty of money to throw around.

Someone called: "What are we going to do when we git there, Sam? Raise potaters?"

Grummond pointed the cane at him. "What are you doing *here,* as far as that goes? Getting rich on nothing a day, nothing a week?" He went on: "There'll be some hungry times, at first. But in the spring them as bends to farming can farm. All you do in that soil is drop a seed and jump out of the way. They'll be stores, pharmacies, hotels. There's a million acres of cattle range for others."

"Only," someone else remarked, "most of it belongs to the

Eighty-Eight Ranch."

"Don't you worry about the Eighty-Eight!" Grummond shot back. "Anybody who stands in the way of the U.P. has got to go. Annie Benson don't pack quite the weight General Dodge does around here."

Grif Holbrook stiffened suddenly. *It can't be Annie,* he thought. *Annie ain't a rancher.*

Yet something told him it was. It would be typical of Annie. Disappear for three years and pop up running a cattle ranch.

He moved to where Grummond was standing. "Maybe this Annie Benson is tougher than we figger," he remarked. "Where'd she come from?"

Grummond shrugged his narrow shoulders. "Californy, I hear. She was mixed up in another ruckus of the same kind. Tried to block Ben Holladay when he was consolidating the stage trails." Grummond tilted his derby with the point of his cane. "I was talking to the general about it this morning," he added importantly. "General Dodge says he's going through next month, sure. I don't think no woman is going to scare *him* out with a broom!"

Grif Holbrook's was the one sober face in the saloon. He said: "You know something? You ain't going to touch a yard o' dirt on Annie Benson's land till I go out and talk to her. Annie's a friend of mine."

The promoter stroked his chin. "So she's a friend of yours!" He was talking loud, for the crowd. "So I let all these investors of mine suffer just because you happen to know her."

Grif's blood, spiked with too much alcohol, came swiftly to a boil. He had Grummond's black stock tie in his fist. He had the seamed face close to his.

"You hear me?" he repeated flatly. "You ain't leaving

Cheyenne till I say you can!"

Sam Grummond's cane whistled. The polished cherry wood struck Grif on the nose. "You damned drunk!" he cried. "I didn't come here to argue with a whisky fighter. I say we leave at sunrise."

Grif Holbrook was drunk, but he could see clearly enough to drive solidly to Grummond's mouth with a punch that dropped the dapper little promoter to the floor. Grif stood over him, breathing through his teeth, bitter with rage.

Sam Grummond was dazed, but he could still yell. "This is your fight, men!" he called to the crowd. "It's your investment at stake!"

Then Grif knew the whisky he had drunk had tricked him. Sober, he would have avoided a fight like this. He'd have caught up with Grummond later.

For a moment the crowd held back, but it would be for a moment only, Grif knew. He braced himself and thought: *Hell! This is as good a way as any. This way they'll at least know what I think of their breed!*

The ones in back were the first to rouse. They started yelling and pushing, then a bald-headed Irishman with a red beard drove forward with his head tucked down.

Grif slugged him, and the man went to his knees. Another tried to get behind him, but Grif caught him by the arm and dragged him back, chopping him on the nose. He stabbed, right and left, at a pair who came in together, and they retreated with bloody faces.

Then the mob surged forward like a tide. . . .

Cheyenne talked about that fight for months, about the burly ex-shotgun messenger who fought until General Dodge's track workers were piled around him like cordwood and puzzled over the things he shouted as he fought: "Keep 'em rolling, boys! There's another empty saddle!" They said it sounded as though he were fighting Indians from the deck of a stagecoach. He went down at last, from a blow from behind. But no one went near him until they were dead sure he was out.

The jail cell was cold, an unheated room destitute of comforts. Grif walked up and down, shivering, thoughts of Annie Benson tracking back and forth through his brain. How had she found her way out here from California? He hadn't forgotten the way she'd left him—lonely and anxious, with just a letter for comfort, a letter that had asked him to wait for her, that said there was too much in the way for them ever to find happiness together.

There hadn't been, but Annie didn't know that. The worthless gunfighter of a husband who had tracked her to California was dead in a gunfight when Annie wrote that. She was the little red-headed widow he had been seeking for years.

Annie, Annie! Grif thought. *Were you just born to trouble?* Last time she owned a link in the transcontinental stage route that she wouldn't sell, and Grif had been sent out to coerce her. This time she was blocking the U.P.

The jailer unlocked the cell door. "Somebody's went your bail," he announced.

"You got the wrong man, brother," Grif said. "Who'd pay an old shotgun messenger's bail in a railroad town?"

"I ain't got nothin' wrong," the jailer insisted. "You're to report to Car Sixteen, on the siding."

Car Sixteen stood in a bitter wind whistling down from the Black Hills, smoke whipping in ragged tatters from its chimney. Curiosity was the motive that sent Grif Holbrook to the siding. All around it stood mountains of material—rusty nails, cross-ties, crates of nuts and bolts. Grif knocked on the door.

The man who opened it was in uniform. He had a bronzed, seamy countenance, dominated by sharp eyes. He said: "Come in, Holbrook."

Grif waited to be invited before he sat down. For this one man, of all the thousands in the railroad army, he had respect. General Dodge was a fighter who knew his own trade of soldiering and who was showing that he was not too old to learn a new one.

The general poured two cups of coffee. With the forefinger of his left hand he held his mustache out of the coffee as he drank. He drank noisily, thumped the cup down.

"That was a corking good fight, Holbrook," he said finally. "I heard about it from Nye, my grade boss."

Grif studied his face. It was as impregnable as a stone fortification. Suddenly Dodge smiled.

"Relax, Grif," he said. "They needed it. Workers get ornery if they aren't kept busy, just like soldiers. I didn't send for you to chastise you. I want to cry on your shoulder."

Grif Holbrook grinned, feeling his muscles relax. Here was a man you could talk to. Here was a man who'd josh with you. "What's the trouble, General?" he asked. "Annie Benson getting in your hair?"

Dodge snorted. "I can take care of Annie Benson. I've had her land condemned. When I'm ready to go ahead, no woman rancher with a handful of cowhands is going to stop me. No, it's something touchier than that. It's man trouble."

The coffee washed some of the aches out of Grif's carcass. He let the general talk.

"I've mentioned my grade foreman, John Nye," Dodge continued. "It's on his account I've wasted three weeks here. Nye's a good man. I couldn't have asked for better all the way from Omaha. But now . . . well, here we sit, while he tears up plan after plan for trestles and fills. I'm beginning to think," the general growled, "that these Black Hills have him whipped." He scowled down darkly into his coffee cup.

Grif scratched his head. "Are they any different from any other mountains?" They were rugged, he knew, and savagely cold. The wind brought carloads of snow down from Canada to frost the peaks like a wedding cake. But the U.P. would have to cross still more inhospitable ranges before it came to rail's end.

"Hell, no!" Dodge exclaimed. "Only they do happen to be the first real mountains we've struck. I've given Nye two weeks to get enough roadway graded to pull the track out of Cheyenne. The men are rotting here, and that fool, Grummond, is proselyting a lot of them."

This came very close to Grif's personal problem. He asked the general about Sam Grummond.

"He knows somebody in Washington, I suppose," General Dodge replied. "The railroad is entitled to alternate sections along the road. In this case, Annie Benson owns the land we're going through. We get around that by condemning a small portion of her land and paying for it. Grummond has bought up a section where he plans to build a city. God knows what the residents will live on!" he added vehemently.

Grif said—"Grummond's a phony."—his face darkening.

Dodge made a gesture of dismissal. "Of course, he is, but he's no worry of mine. When I heard you were in town, Grif, I was damned glad. I knew John Butterfield and Ben Holladay. I know from them that you could talk a rattlesnake into climbing a tree. All I want you to do is to worm into John Nye's confidence and find out what ails him. In the morning he leaves for the hills to do some surveying. You'll go along as his rod man."

So long a time had Grif been drifting without purpose that he hardly understood the upsurge of enthusiasm within him.

He felt warm; he felt about ten years younger. This practically made him a railroad man, of course, but what the hell? He was going back to work!

General Dodge was saying: "I've got to head back to Washington for a couple of months before some lard-bellied Congressman gets my appropriation halved. I'm looking to you to keep me in touch with things."

He sounded tired, Grif thought.

II

There was an odor of liquor on John Nye, and in an office, Grif Holbrook thought, liquor was a bad thing. It made it appear that a man's work did not come first.

Nye stared at him across a drafting board at the back of a car fitted up as living quarters and office. Nye was in his early thirties, a big, lanky man with a hungry look on his face. He had the look of a kid who was growing fast and not getting enough to eat, but his eyes were old—too old for his face.

Grif introduced himself, but Nye did not extend himself to be friendly.

"I've already got a good rod man," he said.

Grif was noncommittal. He sat down in the most comfortable chair in the room. "I dunno," he said. "General Dodge told me to report to you. I used to be with him in the Army."

Nye threw his pencil against the drafting board. "What the U.P. needs," he snapped, "is fewer war veterans and more professional engineers."

Grif's fingertips massaged his unshaven jowls as he inspected the room with a cool glance. "Guess we could set my cot up right over there," he said. "I might as well bunk with you."

John Nye stared at him in silent disgust.

A light footstep sounded on the iron doorsill, and Grif saw a young girl standing there, holding onto the bars at either side of the door. She was a slim, attractive girl with shining blonde hair.

"Oh, hello, Nancy," Nye greeted her. He glanced at Grif, and made a grudging introduction. The girl was Nancy McConnell, daughter of Captain McConnell, who commanded the cavalry detachment the government furnished the railroad in case of Indian trouble.

Grif, standing up, excused himself. "I'll go over to the hotel and get my suitcase," he said.

When he returned, twenty minutes later, the girl was still there. He could hear her voice before he went up the ladder.

"I think it's perfectly idiotic not to take a guard!" she was saying angrily. "You know what happened to that lineman last month."

"He didn't keep his eyes open," Nye answered coldly. "If he'd scouted the cañon before he went up, he'd have known there were Sioux around."

"Just the same," insisted the girl, "Dad's men are just sitting around waiting to be used! You could have a guard for the asking."

Nye said: "They get in my way." After a moment, he added: "I've got a lot of things to clean up, Nancy. I'll see you after dinner."

Grif looked surprised when the girl came out, as though he'd just arrived. He helped her down, and she hesitated a moment before going on.

"Have . . . have you ever fought Indians?" she asked him. It was a naïve question, but he knew what she was getting at.

"I ain't exactly known as the red man's best friend," Grif responded, and grinned. "I can smell Indians six miles away. Don't worry, miss."

Grif Holbrook heard John Nye as he dressed the next morning while it was still dark. It was cold in the car, and Grif was grumbling as he got into his clothes. This Wyoming country always had its cold feet on his back. Los Angeles—that's where he would be heading, someday. You could make a fortune in cattle and sheep—and could ride in your shirt sleeves all winter.

They had breakfast in the mess car and afterward saddled their ponies. In town they found Sam Grummond with ten wagons loaded with men, ready to roll to Antelope and fortune. There was a lot of drinking, a lot of noise. Six great Conestoga wagons were loaded to the tilts with the materials out of which this new El Dorado was to be built.

Sam Grummond sat sprucely in a buggy equipped with side curtains. He stuck his head out through the curtain to say to Grif: "What you got yesterday is just a patch on what you'll get if you interfere with me again. I got papers from the government, and I've got boys to back me up."

Grif looked down at him, despising him. The promoter had the soul of a money-lender, but he was beneath loathing. Grif said: "You bore me, Grummond. Don't get in my way."

Grummond drew his head back, whipping up his horse, and then Grif saw the carbine resting across his knees.

Under a yellow fuzz of buffalo grass the prairie undulated gently. Gaunt knobs of rock, like knuckle bones, protruded through the ground. A cold wind combed the grass. Twenty miles ahead the earth buckled to form a rugged chain of mountains. Track had been laid only half this distance.

When they had been moving for about three hours, Grif saw a thin rag of smoke on the skyline. Immediately he spoke to Nye and reined in. "Reckon Annie Benson is fixing to kill the fatted calf," he observed.

From the crest of a wind-swept rise they could see rail's end below them. A mound of rocks stood like a gray shoulder against it. Beyond the rocks stretched a line of a dozen horsemen, and in the middle of the line Grif saw Annie Benson.

He said to John Nye: "Stick with Grummond. I've got to talk to Annie over there."

He tried to keep the pony to a casual dog-trot, but the closer he got the harder his spurs pressed; at the last, he was loping.

Conscious of sudden movement in the group of cowpunchers, Grif kept his hands clear of his carbine and the half-breed Colt slung under his shoulder as he rode up.

Annie Benson spoke quickly: "It's all right, boys. I . . . I think I know him!"

Grif reined in beside her. He reached for her hand, forgetting to take off his hat, forgetting everything but her name. "Annie!" he blurted. "Gosh!"

She was as beautiful as ever. Small and delicate as a Swiss watch, her hair was a rich auburn, with gold brushed through it. But when Grif looked into her eyes, he saw that the last three years had changed her. Her eyes were sad; more, they were hard, as though they were looking out for Annie Benson, now.

Annie said: "What's happened to you, Grif?"

"To me?" Grif said. Then, remembering, he touched his nose, which a railroad doctor had taped up for him where Grummond's cane had broken it. "A little run-in with Sam Grummond," he mentioned casually.

Annie smiled. "You seem to be my faithful Saint Bernard, Grif. Every time I get in trouble, you're right there to help me." Then she looked at him more intently. "Or are you with General Dodge?"

A sharp-eyed man with the weathered features of an Indian pulled in beside them. "That's a good question, brother," he remarked. "General Dodge's boys stop right back thar by the monument."

Grif looked him over. "I am Dodge's boy, and I ain't Dodge's boy," he stated. "I'm doin' a job for him, but it don't include laying rails. I and a friend of mine are riding across your range today."

"Around," the man corrected him curtly.

"Grif's all right, Lance," Annie intervened quickly. "Lance Parker is my foreman, Grif. Why do you want to cross my land?"

Grummond's buggy was rattling down the slope, the wagons lumbering behind him.

Grif said: "We'll talk about that later, Annie. Grummond thinks he's going to build a town out here somewheres. He brags he's coming right ahead."

He watched the effect on Annie. She could put sternness in her face, but she could not fool Grif. Annie was scared.

Grif said: "Bring your boys up, Parker. Let's talk to 'em."

Twelve against over a hundred—Grif had faced easier odds. The wagons stopped abreast of the line, and Sam Grummond stood down. He crossed his arms with a pompous gesture.

"You men," he announced, "have five minutes to pull out. Then we go through."

"It won't take that long, mister," drawled Lance Parker, "to tell you to go to hell."

Grummond stood looking at his watch. Four minutes and thirty seconds passed, then he mounted the buggy and took up whip. "All right, men!" he cried.

Parker swung a rope three times around his head, building

his loop to the dimensions of the buggy top. He let it settle, and in the same moment he spurred his pony.

Inside the buggy, Sam Grummond let out a startled yell. His horse lay threshing in the traces, and for the moment no one paid much attention to the wagonloads of railroad men. But Grif Holbrook was not easily distracted. And it was Grif who saw the man in the nearest wagon jerk a carbine to his shoulder.

The shot sounded flatly in the prairie stillness, and Lance Parker abruptly went taut as the bullet plucked dust a few yards behind him. The man who had fired levered another shell into the chamber and stood up.

Now Grif had his cheek pressed against the stock of his half-breed Colt. It was an old Dragoon pistol with a rifle stock, in the butt a canteen filled with brandy. A more powerful medicine, however, came from the barrel end.

Grif took the kick of a gun without blinking. He saw the man with the carbine start, saw him try to stand, and then fall forward on the dashboard. Grif's thumb pulled back the hammer.

"Show's over for today, boys," he announced. "Now turn those wagons and start back. All the land you'll find out here is a plot six-by-two."

There were only a dozen guns to turn them back, but Grif's quick action had cooled the bottle bravery they had brought with them from Cheyenne. The wagons wheeled jerkily, and at the top of the ridge halted to wait for Grummond.

The 88 Ranch boys righted Grummond's rig. Sam Grummond, white and shaking, spoke in a voice that was loud and threatening. "All right, widder!" he yelled. "We'll go this time, but we'll be back! And next time we come, it'll be a-smokin'."

III

Annie Benson had had logs hauled from the mountains to build her ranch house. It was constructed like a blockhouse, with shuttered windows and gun-loops. The floor was of hard-packed dirt. The roof was of sod. There were Sioux Indians around here who liked to lob burning arrows onto the roofs of cabins.

At four o'clock the sun dropped behind the mountains; the cool increased. Lance Parker and a 'puncher laid a giant oak log in the fireplace. "She'll burn two days," Parker prophesied, with the appreciation of a man who spends too much time out in blizzards.

They had beef stew for dinner, with the whole 88 crew and Grif and John Nye sitting around the long table. Grif looked at Annie hungrily. Three years—she hadn't got her out of his mind for a week in all that time.

Presently Grif said: "What are you going to do about the railroad, Annie?" The others, by then, were out tending stock, and Nye had gone to the room he would share with Grif.

Annie's chin lifted. "I showed you today what I'm going to do. And the way you pitched in, Grif, I think maybe I'm doing right."

"Sam Grummond ain't the railroad," Grif pointed out. "He's just a city slicker trying to run a sandy on some ignorant railroad workers. When you come up against the U.P., you'll know you've caught a grizzly. You'll have seventy-five troopers to argue with, then."

Annie confronted him impatiently. "Do you think I should let them cut my range up?" she demanded angrily. "Let them bring a swarm of worthless trash to steal my springs and fence off my creeks?"

Grif said: "There's two things you can do. You can sell out, clear a profit, and let somebody else do the worrying. Or you can stay here and see what happens. Either way, the U.P. is coming through."

Annie sounded tired. "What do you want me to do, Grif?"

Grif took her hand. "You've been fighting alone too long. You need a man, Annie. I want you to sell out and go to Californy with me."

Annie's lips tightened. "I ran away from the fight last time, Grif, but now it's caught up with me again. I admit it gets dreadful weary out here . . . no other women, no stores. But this time I'll leave when the job's finished . . . not before." She went on: "You can tell General Dodge he has my permission to go through. I suppose I might as well let him as be forced into it. But the land is still under quarantine, as far as Grummond is concerned."

It was still savagely cold, and barely daylight, when Grif and John Nye left the next morning. There was little warmth in the lemon-yellow sun. They picked their way up a cañon marked here and there with red-capped surveyors' stakes. Behind them trailed a burro carrying a rod-and-chain and other gear.

Nye was poor company. He was silent, brooding, and, when Grif got a good look at his face, he saw that the engineer was sweating. Sweating, with the thermometer at twenty degrees!

Grif had his carbine across his lap. Going without escort into this country was plain foolish.

High in the foothills they halted at a point where the rails would be forced to jump a narrow cañon. Nye said: "This is it."

With rocks, he pinned a blueprint to the ground. Grif looked about and saw that the whole section bristled with stakes. It had been thoroughly surveyed already; by the look of the blueprint, every timber, every bolt, had been charted.

Temper came up in Grif. "Young feller," he snapped, "did you bring me out here to survey something that's already been laid out?"

Nye avoided Grif's glance. "I . . . I'm re-checking," he said at last. "This Chloride Cañon bridge is important. It's sort of a . . . a test. Farther up, we jump Dale Creek Cañon. That will be the highest bridge in the country . . . highest in the world, maybe."

Grif Holbrook said flatly: "Mister, there's nothing wrong with you but buck fever."

John Nye started. "Buck fever?" he repeated.

"You're afraid of starting this thing! If you never built a bridge before, you shouldn't be drawing pay as an engineer," Grif declared bluntly.

Anger swept color into Nye's cheeks, but he made no reply. A frown creased his brow momentarily, then Grif heard the sound—a musical twang, as though Death had suddenly plucked a violin string in the manzanita thicket up the cañon.

Something whizzed between them and struck the cutbank. Grif stared at it. A broken wooden shaft lay at the foot of the bank, one end feathered. The other end had been shredded where the arrow had splintered against the rocks.

Both men started running for the horses. They had the bark of rifles to spur them, now, and the gobbling war cries of Sioux warriors.

They stopped before mounting to fire into the file of bucks stringing down the grade. Nye made Grif ride in front. That was not the act of a coward for the man in the rear would be the first to go. Grif was just beginning to understand his companion.

The trail kept a flank of the hill between them and the Sioux most of the time. What glimpses they had were of straining bodies naked above the waist, of single feathers struck into black warlocks. *No big boys among them, thank God*, Grif thought, *just a party out hunting random scalps.*

They debouched from the cañon into the broken, rock-studded foothills. Looking back, Grif counted eight Indians. One rode far to the rear.

Atop a knoll crowned with boulders, Grif Holbrook dismounted. He was remembering now that the horses were cavalry animals, borrowed from Captain McConnell. They would stay where they were told. Grif showed Nye where he wanted them, then, together, they scrambled up the rocks.

Grif had the Dragoon on full cock now, as the bucks strung up the slope, firing as they came. All but two carried rifles; bandoliers were slung across their breasts. Grif waited until he had a yellow-streaked face in his sights, then fired, knocking an Indian out of his saddle. After that there was no space at all between his shots. His lead, and Nye's, splintered the spearhead until the Indians finally swung aside.

Three of the attackers were down. The others abruptly wheeled and started back up the cañon.

Grif said: "We can make another mile on them while they try to figger out what happened."

On the flats it was more dangerous. There was no place to make a stand now except in an occasional buffalo wallow. Indians rode hard, and would force their ponies until they dropped.

There was, however, no further sign of the war party. This group of braves apparently didn't want scalps badly enough to fight for them.

They jogged on toward the Widow Benson's.

Grif looked at John Nye. Nye was sweating again, and Grif chuckled. "Shake your liver up a little, sonny?"

Nye started. "Oh!" he said. "No, not the Indians. I'm used to them." Then he said: "Grif, you've got 'er figured out right. I'm afraid to build that bridge . . . yellow, if you want to call it that."

Grif nodded. "Sometimes," he said, "if you take a skeleton out of the closet and take a good look at it, you forget you're a-feared of it."

Nye filled his lungs. "Sure," he said. "Sure, I'll talk about it. I'll talk about a bridge I built once before it collapsed. Before forty-five soldiers drowned because of it . . . and me."

Grif didn't know what he had been expecting, but it wasn't this. "When did it happen?" he asked Nye.

" 'Sixty-Four." Nye's voice was flat. "I was with the Engineers. I'd built railroad bridges in Massachusetts before the war, so the Army wanted me to rebuild bridges the Rebs dynamited in their retreat. That meant wooden trestles, and I didn't know much about them. But they all stood . . . except one."

They rode along, Grif silent. This was not something you could simply talk a man out of. This was serious. But Nye suddenly had to talk. The bars were down, and he couldn't stop now if he had wanted to.

"I could draw the plans for that bridge from memory!" he exclaimed suddenly. "It was sound, I tell you! It should have stood against a flood. But the first time a train went over it at high speed, it collapsed."

"Then how in tarnation did you get this job?" Grif demanded in surprise.

Nye shrugged. "That's the Army for you. They never got around to investigating it, as far as I know. General Dodge picked me on my record for assistant B&B man . . . the chief died of yellow fever before we had laid twenty miles of track."

Grif asked the question that had stumped him. "Why in hell did you take it?"

Nye's eyes were fixed on the horizon. "I figured I could prove to myself that it wasn't my fault. That it was . . . a fault in the earth, maybe. But every time I look at that cañon, I get the shakes." After a while he said: "So now you can tell Dodge, Grif, and I'll get fired, and everybody will be happy."

For once, Grif Holbrook had no word of comfort to offer.

IV

They spent the night at Annie Benson's and in the morning rode on to Cheyenne. On the way they passed Sam Grummond's horde, camped on the cheerless prairie. Grif examined the situation from every angle, and from every angle it looked black. He wanted to play square with Johnny Nye; it wasn't good for a man to have a festering sore like that on his conscience. In the end, it would rot his whole being. But there were a few thousand other people's lives at stake in this thing, and a man had to view the case broadly.

Dodge had left for the East by the time they arrived in town. Grif and Nye separated at the spot where the general's private car had stood.

Nye said—"I'll tell the boys we roll out in the morning."—and rode over to the quartermaster corral.

Grif walked to the telegraph shack. There, with a sigh, he did what he had to do, feeling himself without any alternative.

A reply came back from Omaha that night. **Tell that damned fool, Nye, to forget the war and get to work,** read the reply. **According to Secret Service, the Mussel Creek bridge was sabotaged. Does he think I'd have hired him with that on his record?** The wire was signed: **Dodge, Chief of Construction**.

Grif showed the telegram to Nye when he came back from dinner. Nye read it, his brows pulling in. His fist closed slowly over the paper, and for a long moment he stood at the door, staring out into the purple dusk.

"How does the Secret Service know what happened at Mussel Creek?" he murmured finally. "Nobody could tell anything from that tangle of broken timbers. They gave me the benefit of the doubt, that's all."

In disgust, Grif put on his hat and shoved past him. "If a feller wants to waller in misery," he stated, "there's nothing I can do to help him."

In the morning wagons and flatcars were loaded with material, and swampers began to cut into the vast supply dump. A steady stream of mule-drawn iron cars rumbled out of town. Tents were folded, cases of whisky and portable bars loaded, and the spangled finery of the honky-tonk girls exchanged for woolen dresses.

Hell on Wheels was rolling again. In a few months Cheyenne might be remembered only by its headboards, or from the little nucleus of frame buildings a city might start.

They passed Grummond's temporary village. A number of the settlers looked envious; at heart they were all railroad men, and now they had to watch the building of this road when, a few weeks ago, they themselves had been building it. They had exchanged a sure wage for a gamble, and now some of them at least seemed to be realizing they had made a mistake.

There was a fascination in Grif, watching the way the rails built up across the high hills as though coming off a giant reel.

Three miles a day was the goal. Grade bosses went ahead with shovel gangs and scrapers while tie-buckers laid cross-ties upon the brown mole's-burrow. Maul-men spiked down the rails, and iron peddlers distributed joint fastenings to complete the job.

In a few days the little work engine was bucking up the foothills. The line ran only two miles from Annie Benson's ranch house, and now a gaunt skeleton-like framework mounted from the bottom of Chloride Cañon.

It was on a Sunday morning that Grif saw Sam Grummond's buggy rattling off toward the 88 Ranch. Grif caught up with the land peddler a mile from the big, log ranch house. He cocked a knee about the saddle horn and grinned down at the promoter.

"Well," Grif said, "this is real pleasant. I reckon you and me have a little business to finish, Grummond, and right now looks like as good a time as any to finish it."

Grummond's black eyes smoked with anger, but this time he kept a tight grip on his temper. "Bygones are bygones, Holbrook," he declared. "I didn't think you were small enough to hold a grudge against a man for licking you in a fair fight."

"Fair," Grif murmured. "Well, I suppose forty railroaders against one stage man is close enough. But this time I'm going to skin you up on the Widow Benson's account."

"Before you go off half-cocked," suggested Grummond, "suppose you let the Widder Benson decide whether or not she wants to see me. I'm not cat-footin' around. I'm heading straight for the ranch to palaver with her."

The idea intrigued Grif. Annie's tongue had the sting of a bullwhip when she was aroused. This might be fun to watch.

"All right," he said, "drive on, brother. Maybe this'll be worth seein'."

Most of the 88 crew were away when they pulled up at the steps of the ranch house. Annie Benson came to stand on the porch as a young 'puncher came from the harness shed. Sam Grummond dragged a large crate from the rear of the buggy and, grunting under the weight, carried it to the porch.

Annie Benson's eyes were stormy. "Mister Grummond," she said, "I thought I made it plain what was going to happen to you the next time you crossed my land."

Sam Grummond smiled blandly. "Missus Benson," he said, "this is purely a social call. I thought you might be needing a few little things you don't often find out this way."

He was opening the box and pulling out a bolt of red-checkered gingham. He unrolled it casually. Next he exhibited a shiny copper teakettle.

Suddenly Grif Holbrook saw the whole thing. He grabbed Grummond by the scruff of the neck. "Bribery won't help you here!" he snapped. "Back to the buggy with that junk, feller."

But Annie had already glimpsed the treasures—stuff that couldn't be purchased this side of St. Louis. Her voice was agitated. "Oh, let him be, Grif!" she intervened. "I . . . I guess it wouldn't hurt just to take a look."

She let Grummond carry the crate into the parlor. She made tea. Then she sat in a straight-backed chair, her fingers locked together, while he displayed the goods he had brought: a bolt of silk, a bolt of cotton, a bolt of dove-gray wool; a set of copper pans; a self-heating flat-iron; a new alarm clock; and, finally, a stereopticon set to brighten long winter evenings.

Annie looked excited. "What's all this going to cost me?" she asked.

Grummond appeared offended. "Why, nothing, Missus Benson! It's a gift. I just got to thinking that I couldn't sell this stuff anyway, till the boys get settled and bring out their womenfolk. Better you should have it than that it should lay around till moth and rust doth corrupt . . . as the Good Book says."

He started to leave, but Annie halted him in a choked voice. "This . . . this is mighty nice of you, Mister Grummond. I don't quite know how to. . . ."

Grummond made an airy gesture, while Grif stared at him in black hatred. "Don't trouble your mind," the promoter said. "I know how tough such things are to get out here. Of course, if there was a town nearby, you'd always have them on your front doorstep."

He had reached the door now, and Annie halted him again. "Mister Grummond?"

Grummond's eyes were gleaming. In his heart, Grif knew, the fellow was laughing at Annie for her womanly weakness. But he made his voice soft, amiable. "Yes?" he said.

"I was thinking," Annie suggested, "that we might be able to reach some sort of an agreement about this . . . this settlement of yours. I'm a neighborly woman, and I don't particularly enjoy living so far from other folks, especially women. If you could just give me some sort of assurance that your people won't be jumping my creeks and my best range. . . ."

Grummond had a paper in his hand. He flattened it out on the table. "All this needs, ma'am," he stated, "is your signature and mine to put all those desires of yours down in black and white. Antelope will be a benefit to the whole territory. We don't want your creeks, and we ain't got our eyes on your range. This is an irrigatin' country. I'm going to build a dam up in the mountain and bring down water right to our doorstep. We would like to buy some of your less desirable land for farming, though. So if you'll just sign here, Missus Benson. . . ."

Grif gripped Annie's arm so tightly that she winced. "Are

you loco, Annie?" he demanded. "This buzzard is playing your weaknesses! Anybody but a woman could see it. If you sign that, you're signing your own eviction notice a year from now!"

But Annie's eyes wore blinds—blinds of bright calico. She flushed.

"This is my ranch, Grif Holbrook! I reckon I can protect my own interests here."

Grif's hand dropped away. It was worse than a slap. This was his thanks for trailing her all over the West, for taking risks for her, and even a couple of nicks in his hide. He watched Annie accept an indelible pencil from the land peddler and sign the paper; he saw Sam Grummond's signature go down, somewhat shakily, beneath hers.

Grif followed them back to the porch. He stood there a moment, awkwardly, turning his hat in his hands. He said finally: "So long, Annie. I . . . I guess maybe I won't be back."

But Annie didn't hear him. She was pulling her treasures out of the crate and piling them around her feet. . . .

V

Grif had a wind at his back all the way to camp. Gray scud was forming above the mountains, the clouds torn and twisted by cross currents. In the boiling cauldron of the sky, weather was being made. But Grif Holbrook would be heading out of this god-forsaken blizzard range now, certainly before the first screaming storm of winter descended on the plains.

In his tent that night he piled all his gear on a blanket and made a roll. But when the hard night breeze clamped down on the foothill camp, he decided that maybe he could stand one more night here.

Sometime before morning he remembered General Dodge's words to him: "I'm relying on you to keep me posted." That was the last thing the old fighter had told him. And Grif wasn't fooling himself that the John Nye business was by any means cleared up. Conscience—it was a stone you carried in your shoe, a thistle caught in your underwear. But the only way you could get rid of it was to follow its dictates!

Grif stayed on. He watched, from the foothills, settlers swarming onto Annie's range. By the right-of-way they laid out a village of tents and sod houses. It squatted there without visible means of support. By now, perhaps, Annie would be wondering just how the good citizens of Antelope intended to support themselves. They could not all be farmers, and even those who intended to farm would have a year or more to wait before an aqueduct could be constructed.

Grif saw the first snow come, to be melted by a warm Chinook that left the prairie as brown and sodden as an old Army blanket. He was there when Nye supervised the last spike in the Chloride Cañon bridge. Nye drank a pint of whisky in his tent that night.

In the morning, Nancy McConnell visited Grif.

"Father is sending me over to the Widow Benson's to stay," she told him. "Camp is going on up, now that the bridge is finished. It will be pretty rough living for a while. I thought maybe you'd drive me over in the wagon."

Grif hesitated. "Well, I don't know." He had his pride. He wasn't going to go crawling back there—not ever. He was through, now, doing favors for anybody.

Nancy glanced up at the sky. "It looks as if it might snow before I get there," she observed. "You see, Dad doesn't have the authority to detail a guard to drive me over, and I . . . I'm not very good with horses."

The real story was in her eyes, deep and shadowed. She

wanted to talk about John Nye.

Grif said: "Well, I reckon they won't miss me here. I'll hitch up a wagon, miss."

They followed the sandy bed of the cañon to the flats a few miles distant. Nancy McConnell, thought Grif, was a spicy little dish for any man. She was bundled in a heavy plaid Mackinaw with a fur collar. A blanket covered her knees, and she wore fancy, beaded Cheyenne gloves. But down inside all that fur and wool, somewhere, was Nancy, like a sweet kernel, although all Grif could see was her face, pinked with frost. This girl possessed a strong, free spirit that Grif liked, which was why, now, he was going out of his way to help her.

"Mister Holbrook," she said, "we've got to do something about Johnny. Last night I saw him sitting out on the middle of the bridge for three hours. Just sitting there and brooding. I . . . I don't even like to think about what it may mean. . . ."

Grif patted her hand. "Johnny ain't losing his mind," he assured her. "He's got worries." Then he told her about the story Nye had given him that night, and about the wire to General Dodge, and Dodge's reply. "You see," he continued, "there's some sicknesses that have to be burned out by fever, and that's what's happening to Johnny. Maybe after the bridge has been proved up, he'll be fine."

Nancy looked relieved. "Why, if that's all . . . ," she said. "Look here, Mister Holbrook . . . if you'll help me, we can probably have him all right in two days!" Nancy was thinking out loud. "It would take a real test to convince him, of course," she went on. "But why couldn't we do this? Some night, when a new load of iron has been brought up too late to be unloaded, you could jump in the locomotive and start it back down the hill. There'd be enough steam for you to be hitting thirty or forty when you passed the bridge. If the bridge held up under that load of iron, at high speed, Johnny would have to be convinced that his design was sound."

Grif was mentally picturing the cañon. The highest trestle in the United States. . . . "And if it didn't?" he murmured.

"Oh, but there's no question of that!"

Grif turned up his coat collar against the increasingly bitter wind. "With me," he said, "there is a question. I like that young feller. But if he ain't got any more faith in his work than that, I'll let somebody else do the high-wire act." And his jaw tightened stubbornly.

Nancy McConnell saw that his mind was made up. She retreated into her wraps, then, and had no more to say.

The storm had held off too long already. Winter had been growling in his cave for days, and now his gray paws covered the whole sky. Great, downy flakes of snow shook down upon them as they finished the ride, and the southwest wind came at them like a knife.

Activity was noticeable about the 88 Ranch as they drove into the yard. Six saddled ponies stood under the trees, backs humped against the wind. On the long porch, cowpunchers in heavy storm clothes were listening to Annie Benson, who stood in the doorway. The wind, rushing through the bare trees, kept Grif from hearing her words.

They went up the steps, Grif averting his gaze from Annie. He confronted her leathery-faced foreman, Lance Parker. "Looks like war medicine," he said to Parker.

Parker had a woolen scarf tied under his chin, a hat over that. "Them damn' Antelopers!" he snapped. "Rusty seen four of 'em building a sod house on Bear Creek. That's our finishin' pasture. We're going over to roust 'em out."

Annie Benson said—"Grif."—and Grif met her eyes sullenly. He said: "Don't think I've come crawling back here. This girl is Captain McConnell's daughter. She's to stay here with you until the camp is on over the hump."

Annie said, standing aside: "Come in for a minute, Grif."

Grif trudged in. He pulled off his gloves and made a show of thawing his hands before the fire. But Annie held them and made him face her.

"I was a stupid, selfish woman, Grif," she said. "I listened to a hypocrite, and now he's got his foot in the door."

Her eyes melted him. "What's a woman got a man for?" he muttered in a choked voice finally. "I'll take care of Grummond. He's been askin' for this."

"It's not fair," Annie objected. "You take all the risks for me, and get nothing back but ungratefulness. Only I'm making you a promise, Grif . . . come spring, I'll sell out and go to California with you."

Grif Holbrook felt his heart swelling. "I'm going to chisel that on a rock, Annie," he murmured at last. "It'll do for my epitaph. 'He's gone to Californy, with his red-headed widder'." With that, Grif pulled on his gloves. "Well, I'll be riding on over with the boys. And don't you be worrying now."

He had thought the California mountains cold, but compared to this snow-burdened wind that came whooping across the Colorado line, the Sierras had been sultry. He had never been warm-blooded anyway, and this cold was putting icicles in his veins. The horses were kicking through eight inches of snow as they forged up Bear Creek.

They rode in a white, howling void. Grif had no idea where they were, what direction they followed. But these Wyoming cowboys, weaned on melted snow, rode doggedly with their heads tucked in, following sign invisible to Grif.

In about an hour, Lance Parker signaled a halt. Carbines came out of snow-clogged boots, and, squinting, Grif was able to discern a leaf-shaped mound ahead of them. Parker dismounted.

"Stay here," he directed the others. "I'll chouse 'em out."

Close to the cabin, he fired a shot into the screen of burlap that served as a door. The sound was curiously dead in the soft-walled void, and there was no response from the cabin.

A cowpuncher shouted: "There's tracks leading around the back, Lance!"

Parker found them, shallow saucers in the snow that would soon be obliterated. He disappeared, but in a moment was back.

"The damn' fools!" he exclaimed disgustedly. "The horse tracks go south from the corral. Theirs go toward the railroad. Betcha the horses busted loose."

Rusty, the cowpuncher, grunted. "They got froze out. There ain't any wood within ten miles of here."

Parker mounted again. There was a strange awkwardness about him that Grif, for the moment, did not understand. He grasped the situation when the foreman said: "Well, boys?"

The nesters were walking to their death—that was what it amounted to. Dismounted, they were setting out in the middle of a rising blizzard. The men these 88 'punchers had come out here to kill or run out had saved them the trouble.

It was a hell of a way to die, thought Grif. Buried in drifts to your neck—starving, freezing. Apparently the others thought so, too.

"Damn them to hell!" Rusty grunted. "It'd spoil my sleep just knowing they were out here."

They pushed on, with that. Sometimes they nearly lost the tracks, then they would become sharper again. The trail began to loop deceptively to the right. The men were foundering. The tracks struggled up a knoll; halfway to the top, Lance Parker stumbled over the nesters.

There was no knowing what to expect from men of this breed, and the four nesters found themselves looking up into a grim line of .30-30s. Snow dusted them so that only their faces showed clearly. The first movement was when one of the men abruptly sat down. Another began to sob.

Parker commanded them to disarm and four revolvers fell into the snow at his horse's hoofs. He said: "We're taking you in on your word to head back to Cheyenne as soon as the storm lifts. If we find you around after that, you'll know what to expect."

There were no arguments, nothing but a stumbling rush for the horses. Grif helped a frost-bitten squatter up behind him. He could feel the man shaking with a chill that rattled his teeth.

"Damn that Grummond!" the man exploded, when he could talk finally. "We paid him a hundred dollars for a cord of wood to be delivered three days ago. I've got my craw full of him and his pipe dreams. I'm signing on with General Dodge the first time a gang car goes by."

With the storm at its peak, they rode into Antelope. The town shuddered under the gigantic draft of the blizzard. Nothing remained of the tents but a few poles and rags. Smoke tore from the chimneys of the sod houses and the half dozen frame buildings. The nesters stumbled toward the largest frame building, on the false front of which was painted a single word: **Merchandise**.

Grif paused to thaw his frozen innards with a drink from the canteen in the bosom of his gun. When he started for the store, he saw that Lance Parker and the others were following him.

VI

There was trouble in Sam Grummond's little paradise. Grif saw that at a glance. Grummond, the center of an angry vortex, stood with his back to an oil barrel that had been fashioned into a stove. A big Irishman with the shoulders of a bear leveled a finger at him.

"We don't want talk this time, Sam, we want facts," the Irishman declared bluntly. "What are we going to live on out here? How are we going to get through the winter? Why didn't you plan on storms before you brought us out here?"

Grummond's black eyes were busy. They were sorting through the crowd, singling out the men he could count on from those he could no longer trust.

"You knew what you were going into, Sheedy," he blustered. "I told you there'd be tough times. But if you'll string with me till spring, you can thumb your nose at railroad work."

There was movement in the crowd as the man who had ridden with Grif reached Sheedy's side. In the light, blotchy patches of frostbite were visible on his nose and cheeks. He asserted: "Here's four that ain't stringin' with you, Grummond! If it wasn't for the Widder Benson's cowpokes, we'd be out there now, froze to death! Where's that wood you promised us?"

Grummond turned accusingly on the Irishman named Sheedy. "You can ask Sheedy about that. I gave him the wood-hauling contract."

Sheedy's hands worked. "For a thousand dollars!" he gritted. "But you didn't give me any wagons to haul it with."

You could almost admire Grummond for his ability to squirm out of a hole, Grif thought. Grummond remained cold; his voice became vitriolic.

"Milksops!" he taunted. "That's what you are, the whole kit an' caboodle of you! You want all the whisky without the labor of pulling the cork! I see now where my plans were wrong. I counted on men, instead of boys in knee pants! Well, the softies always get weeded out, anyway. I'm glad it's come to a head this early." He gave the crowd a long, scornful look, then resumed: "Anybody that's afraid to string with me can step forward right now. I'll see that the first supply train to go through takes you up to the road camp."

For a few moments, his contempt held the men in line. Then Sheedy, with the resourcefulness of an old section boss, strode to the far wall. "Every man that's got a brain in his head," he declared, "line up here to go back to work!"

After that, the factions began to sort out, and, when it was finished, a bare half of the men were still with Grummond. But Grif, looking at him, thought he saw more of triumph in the promoter's expression than defeat.

Grif stepped back into the street, grinning. "Gents," he announced, "we'd just be wasting ammunition on 'em. We've got a bigger gun than General Grant ever owned . . . *winter!* Give them time . . . but keep your eye on them."

The railroad butted on through drifts that deepened with every fresh fall of snow. Dale Creek lay ahead of them—a ragged knife-slash one hundred and thirty-five feet deep.

John Nye began tearing up plans again, but Grif Holbrook could do nothing more constructive than sit by the stove in the box car and drink coffee laced with rum. When Nye had thrown away his sixth plan, Grif made himself a promise: Nye had one more week. After that a wire to General Dodge would put a man in charge who built bridges of wood and iron—not out of pen and ink and paper.

On the first clear day, Annie Benson and Nancy rode up. Annie seemed to have something on her mind. She sat in the car, warming her hands. "Sometimes," she remarked, "I think that man Grummond is crazy. He was over again yesterday. He wanted to buy me out."

"If you didn't horsewhip him off the ranch," Grif growled, "it must have been because you were alone."

Annie said: "It was. He has the confidence of a brass monkey. Said he needs room to expand."

The pool was beginning to clear; Grif could see a little writing on the bottom now. He asked Annie: "What did he offer?"

"About half of what it's worth," she replied. "When I refused, he began to threaten. He said the paper I signed gave him the right to prove up on any creeks and springs the town needs to supply its inhabitants with water. He said I'd have to sell out to him eventually."

Annie was worried. She could talk defiantly and scornfully, but now anxiety showed through these defenses, and Grif patted her shoulder.

"Grummond's done," he comforted her, "only he don't know it yet. Every day another five or six of his men drift in here, hunting work. Old Man Winter's about got him whipped. We'll just set tight till the rats all desert the ship."

Annie said—"I hope so."—but she didn't sound convinced.

Grif pushed Sam Grummond to the back of his mind. Grummond's horse had carried him about as far as it was going to. He was much too occupied with what was going on in Dale Creek Cañon to worry about a four-flushing land peddler. Johnny Nye had finally approved a bridge design. The trestle was going up!

The last surveyor's stake had been pounded in; the concrete piers were sunk, and from the slot-like crevasse slender arms of creosoted timber thrust upward. Nye was everywhere during construction, checking, measuring, riding his men sternly. But Grif knew that behind all his industry was a sharp, small voice called fear. *Keep busy*, it said, *and you won't*

*have time to think. You'll forget about the Mussel Creek bridge,
about forty-five men who drowned under that other bridge you
built. . . .*

Grif was out on the trestle with him the day they began to
lay cross-ties. When he looked down through the spidery
framework, he wanted to reach out and hold onto something.
Far below, the creek was a blue thread traced through the
white abyss of the cañon. The black shadows of the bridge
sprawled down the cañon side like a tangle of wrecked timbers.

An iron wagon stopped at the far end of the bridge. Three
men climbed down and came haltingly down the catwalk.
Nye straightened to stare at them.

"Those fools," he exclaimed, "are drunk! I don't know
what they want, but they're going to get their time."

When the trio reached Grif and John Nye, they stopped,
one of them stepping forward as spokesman. He held his hat.
By his tar-stained clothing, Grif judged him to be a
tie-bucker.

"Mister Nye," the man began in a maudlin voice, "us
three have been miserable sinners. We deserted the road
when it needed us. But we've paid the price, and now we're
broke. We just come to tell you we'll all sign contracts to stick
with you till the last rail is spiked."

Nye looked them over, the angle of his jaw softening a little. He needed workers, and these men had been entitled to
the few drinks they'd had. He nodded to them curtly.

"All right, tell the paymaster I said to put you back on your
old jobs. But we're withholding ten percent of the pay of the
men who quit on us and then come back. You'll get the rest
when the road is finished."

The men consulted. The spokesman faced John Nye
again. " 'S fair enough," he announced thickly. "You'll have

no more trouble out of us, and that's a promise. We've had our bellies full of Grummond's talk of easy money. He's crazy, that's what he is."

One of the others said: "Faith, and I think he's as drunk on greed as another man might be on good whisky! He was talking last night about the Benson woman. 'She's a millstone about our necks, dragging us down to ruin!' he says. 'She's got to go, men!' he tells us, by grabs!"

Nye said gruffly: "All right, men. But remember, you asked for it. Now go sober up and come to work in the morning."

The spokesman said—"Yes, sir."—and stepped back. One of the other workmen yelled, but the warning was too late. The man's foot was off the catwalk; he was dropping between the ties with a scream, his fingers for one instant gripping whitely the edge of the tarred plank. Then he was gone, and, where he had plunged through the trestle, nothing remained but the lingering, hoarse cry of a man going to his death.

Grif shot out a hand to steady Nye, whose face had suddenly gone ashen. But he shook off Grif's hand. He stared up into the sky for a moment, his eyes closed, fists clenched. Then he walked rapidly away from the bridge.

After they had recovered the body of the tie-bucker, Nye put on a Mackinaw and hiked up the grade, past the farthermost workers. Grif saw his gray-and-red checked Mackinaw as a bend in the trail cut him off, a half mile up the cañon. He didn't try to follow.

At dark the engineer was still not back, and Grif began to worry. He knew how terribly the death of the workman had shaken Nye. He realized that John Nye's mind would put it down as an omen of ill luck, that Nye might figure it as a black mark against the bridge before the span was even completed.

At nine o'clock Grif got into his heavy sheepskin storm

coat and followed Lance Parker's trick of wrapping a woolen muffler around his head and pulling his hat down over it. The night was like blued steel; not a wisp of cloud marred it.

Grif was heading for the quartermaster corral to saddle his horse when he heard a sound at the bridge.

VII

The entire camp, for a distance of several hundred yards above and below the bridge, was posted. There was no interior guard, however. Grif knew it was not a picket he had heard at the bridge. He had the stock of his gun in his right hand as he paced through the frozen snow.

Standing there at the edge of the trestle, he sorted the small sounds coming to him. Suddenly he turned. He could see, not twenty feet away, the form of a man crouching at the base of a timber beneath the bridge, just below the bank.

He spoke sharply. "All right, feller! Come out, or I'll blow you out of your boots."

He was taking up trigger slack when the man straightened. "Grif?" he called up in a low voice.

It was Nye. And this was how Grif had feared it might be. Nye was not going to have that bridge collapsing. He was going to destroy it and then get to hell out of there.

Nye came up the bank. His face was like the snow—hard, white, pitted with shadow. He said: "What did you expect of me? I told you I was yellow, didn't I?"

Grif said: "I didn't believe you. But now I'm convinced. I'll wire Dodge in the morning."

Grif did not move until Nye had started back to the car they shared. Then he kept beside him.

"I've fought it, Grif," Nye groaned, "but it's in my guts all the time, like a cold rock."

A picket's challenge came to them from downcañon. They could not hear the reply, but the sentry called: "Advance and be recognized!" A moment later he shouted—"Corporal of the guard . . . post Number Two!"—in the traditional cry of the sentry who has sensed trouble.

Grif Holbrook ran down the roadway with Nye behind him. From the guard tent, a yellowish pyramid of lighted canvas, ran the corporal, revolver in hand. They were close behind him when he reached the picket at the lower fringe of the camp.

"What's the trouble, Morrissey?" the corporal demanded.

Private Morrissey held his rifle at the port. "A man's down over yonder!" he answered excitedly. "He was coming up the road, but stopped when I challenged him. I could hear his spurs, but he was afoot. Said his name was Parker. Then he stumbled and went down."

Parker! The name went into Grif like a knife thrust. He spoke to the corporal. "I've got some whisky. Maybe we can bring him around."

It was Lance Parker who lay crumpled on the frozen ruts of the wagon road, his blood-crusted hand clutching at the iron-hard mud. His eyes were open when they raised him, and he drank some whisky from Grif's canteen.

He was looking at Grif, struggling to speak. His voice came in a painful, panting whisper finally. "You were right, mister," he gasped out. "The winter whipped Grummond, but he ain't got sense enough to know it. He's raidin' Annie Benson tonight!"

The words resounded in Grif's ears. *He's raiding Annie Benson.* The tie-bucker who had died that day had told them Grummond was preaching retaliation on Annie.

He could read the writing now. Grummond's last chance

was to run Annie out with force. Maybe it had been his plan from the beginning. Maybe Antelope was just a magnet to draw a worthless crew of killers to him. He had a wild-eyed army of thirty or forty men left, which meant he could take the ranch without too much trouble.

Grif made Parker drink some more whisky. "How did you get out?" he demanded. "How long ago?"

"I got out of the cabin about seven." Parker's voice was steadier now. "Somebody clipped me as I ran. They were all over the yard, but I shot one and got his horse. I rode it until it dropped. I . . . I don't know how far I walked."

Grif asked Parker how many men had attacked the ranch, but Parker had done all his talking for a while, and they carried him into camp. A sharp urgency drove through Grif. *How do we get there before they break in? My God, that crew would treat the women like Cheyennes!*

The guard detachment was cavalry, not infantry. But even cavalry might not make it across the foothills in time. Yet there was one other way. The cavalry would not like it—a trooper dismounted is always a complaining trooper—but it would put them hours ahead.

"Let's go talk to Captain McConnell," Grif said shortly.

McConnell, chief of the guard detachment, was a sour-eyed Scotsman who had held a colonel's brevet in the war and was not enjoying his present command. In his freezing tent he pulled on his shirt and pants as the listened to their announcement.

He knew Grummond's attack had put his daughter's life in jeopardy, but he took the news stolidly. When Grif came to the part about loading the troops on the train, he snorted.

"Put my troops into the field dismounted?" he cried angrily. "Not while I can wave a saber! You can ride your damned Puffing Billy down the grade, but I'll be there at the bottom to meet you." It was the voice of the cavalry speaking—the voice of all troopers who could never believe in anything faster or better than a fine horse.

John Nye went white, thinking about four unloaded flatcars of iron that could not be derailed, about the weight of seventy-five men and their heavy fighting equipment, and of a certain bridge over Chloride Creek. . . .

Grif met the captain's eye boldly. "What's the matter with your men?" he demanded. "Are they soft? Any infantryman I ever knew would walk, crawl, or swim to get to a fight! Maybe you'd like us to furnish buggies for your boys."

Color came up from the cavalryman's collar, and part of it was shame. He belted on his Colt. "Stoke up your damned engine!" he exploded. "My men can walk on their hands and still outfight any foot soldier you ever knew!"

But Grif knew Nancy McConnell had won the argument for him. The captain had no desire to stake his stubborn belief in the efficiency of the cavalry against his own daughter's life.

In the warm, fire-lit cab of the locomotive, Grif helped the engineer and fireman heave ironwood into the furnace. Sergeants were dressing up lines of grumbling troopers beside the four rail-laden flatcars that would carry them. Carbine clanked against saber, boots crunched on the hard snow.

Captain McConnell made a speech. "I understand there has been some grumbling about fighting dismounted," Grif heard him declare. "Maybe you men think you're too good for infantrymen. The government pays you two dollars a month more because you've got calluses on your hunkers instead of on your feet. That's the only difference I know of. Let me ask you this. Who stopped Jeb Smart at Gettysburg . . . the infantry or the cavalry?" He let it sink in, then sharply barked the command: "Mount!"

Just before the troop train got under way, Nye swung into the cab. He carried a carbine, with a bandolier slung across his shoulder. He climbed to the top of the wood in the tender in order to see the track. Grif crawled up beside him just as the brakes were released and the train started down the grade.

They began to gather speed at the first comparatively straight stretch. The grade warped through sharp turns on steep mountainsides, followed twisting, snow-choked cañons. Huddled in his overcoat, John Nye sat staring straight ahead. He had Nancy on his mind, and he had the bridge.

Grif had thought Nye a fool to worry about the Chloride Cañon trestle, but as they went clattering on, he now found a heavy strain of fear in himself. Perhaps Nye was right about the Mussel Creek disaster, perhaps he *had* been at fault. . . .

They angled along a forested hillside. Now the timber opened up and Chloride Cañon fell away below them. They were suddenly conscious of the speed of the train. It was steaming along faster than any train had a right to on track that had not been shaken down.

Nye turned to yell at the engineer. "Brake her down, you fool! You'll peel the rails off the cross-ties!"

The engineer, his features ruddily highlighted, looked as frightened as Nye. He made a gesture to indicate that the brakes were already on, that the rails were iced over so badly that he had no traction.

They were on the approach, then, with the wheels hammering at the roadbed. The sound changed suddenly to a hollow, deafening clatter. The bridge was under them, a slim structure of wheel flanges against rails rose deafeningly.

Then there was a crackling under Grif Holbrook, and he was thrown against the side of the tender. He was too frightened to yell. He lay crumpled against the iron side of the car with Nye's weight on top of him, and all that was in his mind was Annie.

VIII

Something was wrong with this wreck. It wasn't noisy enough. The empty drumming of the trestle had given way to the solid grumble of a graveled roadbed. Grif heard John Nye laughing with hysteria just behind the sound.

"The joke's on us, Grif!" Nye was crying exultantly. "The fire wood slipped under us, on the turn. The bridge stood. Did you hear me? *The damned thing is solid as a rock!*"

Grif crawled out, looking like an old brown bear whose sleep had been interrupted. "Maybe you'll stop crying on my shoulder now," was all he said, and settled into a frowning silence that soon infected Nye. The hardest part of the trip still lay ahead of them.

Beyond Chloride Cañon the grade leveled off and gradually the locomotive's drive rods slowed their frantic clanking. They coasted down through the foothills with the steam and smoke of the engine's passing drifting away opaquely on the track behind them.

In this thin Wyoming air, sound traveled with the sharpness of a telegraph. When they disembarked two miles from the 88 Ranch, a patter of shooting reached them. It ceased, but presently other shots sounded. The shots were reassuring to Grif. It was still a fight—not a massacre.

Captain McConnell started his men across the thin snow in squad columns. Grif and Nye walked beside him, at the head. Grif was remembering the lay of the land about the ranch house. Low hills fenced the ranch in on all sides, ren-

dering the buildings vulnerable to an attack. But they could
also act as a noose to trap the attackers.

He told the captain what he remembered of the terrain.
Before the last barricade of hills, McConnell held a war coun-
cil with his lieutenant and the senior sergeants. He was imagi-
native enough to defy tradition by splitting his force. Half of
the detachment he sent west, to take the ranch from the rear;
the other half he led east, to complete the ring.

They reached a height from which they could see the
buildings, dark against the snow. They could pick out Grummond's crowd, deployed around the cabin, by the flashes of
their guns, the dirty, half-drunken remnants of the army he
had brought to Antelope in the fall. These were the ones who
figured they had nothing to lose and all to gain by sticking
with him. There was little shooting, now—a salvo from
Grummond's men, and then a shot or two from the cabin.

Grif knew then that ammunition must be running low in
the big, log fortress. He thought: *This can be complicated, or it
can be easy. No use in a lot of blood spilling.* And there was a little selfish thought, too. He said to the captain: "Grummond
won't want a fight, Captain. He only wants a pushover. Let
me take him your command to surrender. He'll come around
pronto."

"He'll probably murder you," McConnell said dryly, "but
if you want to try it, I won't stop you."

Then McConnell told him to wait. He supervised the de-
ploying of men so that they could put down a brutal fire upon
the thin line of men around the ranch house. He came back in
fifteen minutes. "All right," he said. "It will have to be by
voice signals. If he refuses, you can start back, but I don't give
you much chance to make it. If he agrees, shout the word."

Grif did not notice John Nye until he was halfway down
the slope.

Nye did not slow his stride. "I'm right with you, Grif," he said.

"Maybe you won't be," Grif snapped, "after the ruckus starts. I can take care of myself, but I ain't taking out any insurance on you."

They were within a hundred feet of the cottonwoods where Grummond's men lay in a thin, curving line. Grif halted. "Then lie flat," he directed, "while I try to find Grummond. Keep hid while we talk. Afterward, you're on your own."

It was quiet just then, and Grif's voice rolled through the trees and up against the opposing hills.

"It's Holbrook, Grummond! I'm carrying the white flag. If you're not as gutless as I think you are, you'll step out here."

Silence flowed in after the echoes, then Grummond broke it himself. "I ain't as gutless, maybe," he called out, "but I'm a whole lot smarter, Holbrook! Walk right in. You'll find me."

Grif laid a hand on Nye's shoulder. "So long, sonny," he said.

The shadows hung straight down from the trees, black and cold. Grummond rose like a wraith from a buck brush thicket. He met Grif beside a tree. Two of his men flanked him.

"I never was one to carry bad news," said Grif, "but I've got to tell you that you're surrounded."

Grummond's ugly, wrinkled face broke into lines of sly amusement. "Surrounded by you, Holbrook?" he sneered.

"Surrounded," Grif answered flatly, "by Captain McConnell and seventy-some troopers. They're going to raise hell with you if you don't walk up the slope with your hands high. You've got five minutes to start."

"You can't bluff in this game," Grummond stated carefully. "The cards are down. I'm saying for you to raise your hands. You're my prisoner."

Grif turned his head a little, studying the man. "Do you remember," he asked him, "the night you broke my nose with your cane? I guess I never forgot that. But mostly I ain't forgot how you double-crossed Annie Benson. Annie's a good friend of mine, Grummond. That's why I got McConnell's permission to come down here. I knew you'd never surrender. I came down to kill you."

Sam Grummond's rifle was already in his hands. He was lining it up on Grif Holbrook as Grif brought the half-breed Colt up from under his coat.

Grif was almost blinded by the flash of Grummond's rifle. He fired the Dragoon and heard Sam Grummond grunt. He fired again and saw him stagger back against one of his men.

Grif charged into the other man, shoving the pistol against his belly and firing. At the same time he was yelling: *"Let 'er go, Captain!"*

Long before the troopers closed with them, Sam Grummond's whisky-scented crew broke. They were off-scourings of the track gangs, not soldiers. They came out with their hands up, or they tried to escape and were shot down.

Someone came out on the porch, someone who called: "Grif! Grif Holbrook!"

Grif struggled to his knees. "Right here, Annie!" he said. "You . . . you all right?"

Annie's laugh had tears behind it. "Of course, I'm all right!" she exclaimed in a choked voice. "I knew you'd bring help, sooner or later." Then she said severely: "And now, Grif Holbrook, you get up out of that snow and come in by the fire. You'll catch your death of cold. A man your age, taking chances with his health thataway!"

The Buckskin Poppers' War

I

All morning the stage had been climbing. The oak country had given way to walnut and elm, and these had merged into digger pine and cedar. From suffocating heat they had mounted to coolness. The pines were growing taller. Along some of the streams they saw men panning gold or working rockers; on far hillsides could be seen the scars of placer diggings.

At Rattlesnake, the stage stopped for a fresh team. All the passengers except Grif Holbrook and the girl hurried into the station for a shot of whisky while the team was changed. When the conductor's tin horn called the passengers back, Grif said: "I reckon I'll ride up on top the rest of the way, Miss Katie. Kind of like to study this country."

"Of course." Katie Gillison smiled.

Grif mounted to one of the seats behind the box. Just for a moment he felt a pang of loneliness. He was a long way from Wyoming, a long way from Annie. He hadn't written since he left Los Angeles, because he didn't want to upset her. She thought he was getting established on the big cattle ranch they had been talking about for years, and here he was in the Mother Lode country with a half interest in a stage line he'd never seen! For Grif had made the same discovery a lot of other men who had come to California had made: that the good land wasn't cheap, and the cheap land wasn't good. The profits from his year of trouble-shooting for the Union Pacific would have bought chips in nothing but a goat ranch. He started wandering upstate, looking for some hard-up rancher willing to sacrifice pride to cash.

It was in Sacramento that he found Katie Gillison. She had come out from St. Louis to operate the stage line an uncle had left her. At Sacramento, she told Grif later, she had suddenly realized she was about to jump into something she knew nothing about. That was why she had advertised for a partner to go up to Indian Valley, in the Mother Lode country, to share the work and profits of a short-line stage outfit. Grif took the job. He wasn't cut out for cattle anyway, he decided. If there was some place they were still running the Concords, that was the place for him.

They topped a ridge and swung down a long grade into a dog-leg valley. The warm air was heavy with pitch pine and balsam. Below them the valley was set out neatly. A creek swung down the center of it with just enough room on each side for alfalfa and truck fields.

Grif heard the guard say to the driver: "My Gawd, look at the creek! Thick 'n' brown as restaurant gravy!"

The driver was young and lanky, with blond hair and dark skin. He wore a pony-skin vest over a faded Army shirt. "Purty! But there'll come a day," he remarked cryptically.

The stage ran on with clucking of sandboxes and jingling trace-chains. Curiosity moved Grif to hunch forward and put a conversational foot in the door.

"Little hydraulicking going on?" he asked.

"A little," said the driver. He took the ribbons in one hand and, pulling a plug of Navy tobacco out of his pocket, bit off a corner and passed it to the guard.

"I thought," Grif mentioned, "that gravel mining was illegal."

"Some places it is," the driver grunted. He put the brown

tile of tobacco away.

"Reason I'm curious," Grif volunteered, "I'm taking over a business in Indian Valley. Nothing like knowing your neighbors, is there?"

The driver allowed there wasn't. Neither he nor the shotgun messenger enlarged on this, and the Concord came to the bottom of the grade and struck through blue-green stands of alfalfa toward the wide, brown stream. They stopped where the road dipped into a ford. The driver stood up, spat several times, and sat down.

"We'll give her a try." The leaders stepped into the thick race of roiled water. The stage progressed heavily through the soft mud on the bottom.

Grif was still determined to loosen the driver's jaw. "Matter of fact," he said cheerfully, "I may be giving you boys some competition. I and the lady inside are taking over the Mountain Stage Line."

The driver hitched around to stare. He could have been handsome, except for the scowl under his brows. His face had been formed without too much regard for symmetry, but it went together—square chin, long nose, heavy brows—a kind of face for outdoor work. "What the hell do you want to do that for?" he demanded.

Grif smoothed down the hackles of his temper. "Why," he said, "staging has done right well by me. Sure, I know the talk is all railroads, but I figure it this way . . . these Californy mountains are the last place they'll lay iron. The rails can't catch up with one camp before the boys are whooping off over the hills to another." Then he looked at the man squarely and stated: "That's fine talk, anyway, coming from a stage man."

The other's eyes became slightly less corrosive, but he kept a stubborn tongue. "I'll go along with you on the stage talk, pardner, but I want no part of anybody that toadies to the hydraulickers. Think twice before you sink a dollar in the Mountain Stage Line."

The guard was suddenly pointing with his shotgun. "Great Day!" he yelled. "They're sluicing today for sure! We'll have to go with 'er!"

The creek came through a little grove of oaks just above them, following lazy California turnings, pausing at each bend to hollow a little cove under a bank where trout could hide. But what was coming down the streambed now would choke a trout with silt, and instead of flowing easily through the turns, it was piling against them and tearing great chunks of earth away, leaping over the lower banks to sprawl across the fields and then rejoining the main stream to rush upon the ford.

Somewhere a débris-formed dam had gone down. A flash flood was the result. The driver cracked the whip out, brought the leaders around, and started the stage downstream, hoping to ride out the foaming head and swing back for shore.

Grif was thinking of the girl inside, but all he could do was hang onto the grab-irons and wait, while the water smashed into the back of the Concord and sent a jolt down the tongue that threw three of the horses to their knees. The driver fought the rest, trying to hold them in while the others got up.

The water was pouring into the stage through the windows. The stage was faltering, lurching this way and then back. It was getting ready to go, with the horses down in a wild tangle and the panels coming broadside to the current. Men were trying to smash the doors open, but the water pressure locked them tight.

The driver stood up. He told Grif: "Don't get away from the stage. Hang onto her unless she starts rolling. This muck will fill your clothes and drag you down."

He stood up, perfectly cool, and Grif had the thought as the Concord went over that here was a nice enough young fellow, if he weren't so damned pig-headed.

Grif jumped upstream. When he came up, he had the sensation of having had his clothes turn to lead. They were pulling him down, miring his feet in the mud. He took laborious steps and grabbed a step place of the overturned stage. Heads were sticking out of the windows and door. It might have been humorous if Death hadn't been cracking his knuckles off-stage. The women's bonnets were limp; the men were hatless, their clothes sodden.

Then the water was gone, dropping away as though it had found a hole in the creek bottom. The horses got up; the shotgun messenger and driver were having their time with them. Grif said a word to Katie and went to help them.

It was an hour before the stage was ready to travel. Then the air was getting cool, and it wasn't so pleasant up on the deck. The road found its way out of the valley into a big, darkening basin. Farms spotted the valley, each with its little colony of trees.

Just before they entered Indian Valley, the guard spoke to Grif. "Nice business, eh?"

There was a challenge in his voice. Grif said: "Tough. Why don't somebody stop them, if it's the hydraulic raising all that hell?"

The guard said: "You're a stranger, here, mister, and I reckon I'm just as strange to you. In fact, the whole situation is strange. So I'm going to make a speech. I'm going to say what any man in Indian Valley would say if he knew you were going to start a stage line to High Town. My name's Matson. You see me working, not because I have to, but because I like to. I own this stage and a dozen just like it, and I call the outfit the Sierra Stage Company. I operate between Auburn and Cedar City."

"And," Grif said, "you don't want any competition." His opinion of this man began to change. He was a braggart and a loud-mouth.

"To hell with competition," said Matson, and spat. "The Mountain Line wasn't competition, anyway, even before old man Gillison died. His franchise was only good between Indian Valley and High Town. Of course, Ed Broderick would kiss you on both cheeks if you started a stage service up to the mines. But I don't take his trade, so I wouldn't lose a dollar's worth of business there. What I'm telling you, mister, is that, if you don't want to get shoved off the sidewalks in Indian Valley, don't even look like you *might* shake hands with Broderick."

He said it with a scowl that, to Grif, was comical. Grif leaned forward. "Gosh!" he said. "Are they pretty tough up here?"

Matson said crisply: "I've shown you the chuckholes. It's your fault if you hit 'em." He turned back to stare straight ahead down the street they had entered.

II

In a three-dollar room at the National Hotel, Grif unpacked his grip and selected the most presentable articles for a change. There was a bathroom at the end of the hall, where he sluiced off the mud. The wife of the hotel manager fixed up Katie with some oversize clothing. Taken in here and there with pins, the outfit didn't look at all bad when Katie came into the dining room to find Grif. All the men in the place looked around at her; she had the combination of dark hair, fair skin, and blue eyes that usually turns men's heads, and with it she had a neat little figure to keep them turned.

They had venison steak, fried potatoes, and coffee. After the long ride, and the dousing, the man-size helpings did much to restore Grif's soul. But Katie ate little.

"Don't you like venison?" Grif asked her.

"It's fine. Maybe I'm a little scared and homesick. This isn't much like Saint Louis. I keep wondering what I'm doing out here, anyway. I could have sold everything through the lawyer and just stayed home."

"You'll never get rich prospecting in your back yard," Grif declared. "Tomorrow you'll take a deep breath of this mountain air and decide you never want to leave."

Katie looked dubious. "But tonight we've got to find the lawyer and start straightening things out." She said suddenly: "Oh, I hope it's as good as it sounded in the letter."

Grif patted her hand. "It's going to be the sweetest set-up you ever saw. Finish your coffee, now, and we'll get started." For the time being, he reckoned, Matson could go unmentioned.

The lawyer's name, Katie said, was Muldrow. They found his office upstairs over the bank. Lawyer Muldrow was a small man with a pepper-and-salt stubble on his rutted face.

"Yep?" he said.

Grif made the introductions, and Muldrow invited them in.

"Been looking for you," said Muldrow. "You folks et? Well, have a cup of coffee, anyway."

He ate on his desk blotter, setting cups of blue-black coffee on opposite corners of the desk for the others. He shuffled papers around while he ate. "Yep," he said. "She's all probated. Wants nothing but your signature."

"And just what is there? The stage line and . . . ?"

"Well, let's go through it. 'One house of four rooms, known as the Jenkins house, corner North Street and Third, containing the following furnishings. . . .' We'll skip that for the time being. 'The firm known as the Mountain Stage Line, comprising thirty-six horses, two Abbott and Downing stage-coaches, one main office and stable in Indian Valley, one swing station at Strawberry Cañon, one stable and office in High Town.' That's it. The stage ain't been operatin' lately, you understand. But the stage is here in town. The horses . . . well," he said, chuckling, "I guess a big, stout fella like you can gentle 'em down." Then he leaned back, touching his fingers together, sobering. "I suppose you know about the social standing of the Mountain Stage Line?"

Katie glanced at Grif. "Why," she said, "I don't know that I do. . . ."

Muldrow got up and poured coffee, and, when he sat down again, he gave, as tactfully as it was in him, the same story Matson had delivered on the stage. "You will have more than hard looks to fight, prob'ly. Matson has an idea High Town can be starved out, in time. He may raise a little Cain with you, if you give Ed Broderick any comfort."

Katie was stunned. She looked at Muldrow, then at Grif. "What can I say, Mister Holbrook? Except that I didn't know . . . truly I didn't! I'll refund your money just as soon as I can sell. . . ."

Grif was thinking about the way Matson had said: *I've shown you the chuckholes. It's your own fault, if you hit 'em.*

"You ain't going to sell that road, Katie Gillison," he told her. "I've bought in, and I've got an equal say. I think I can show Mister Matson one or two tricks I picked up with Butterfield and Holladay. I want to talk to this Broderick, too. When you hear so much bad about a man, there must be a little good they're forgetting."

Katie's chin went up. "Oh, I wasn't thinking of quitting! I just thought I might sell the house and repay you, if you want to get out without risking your money. I think I'd like to go back to the hotel now."

But on the way back she suddenly stopped. They were before Matson's Sierra Stage office. "You know," she said, "there's no reason why we should start right out fighting him. Mister Matson might listen to me, where he wouldn't to you." She made some little dabs at her hair, smiled at Grif, and walked inside.

Grif strolled down to a saloon and had a beer. A minute or two after he came out, Katie reappeared. She was walking with quick, little, short-tempered strides, her head high and her fists clenched.

"He may be a business man," she declared, "but he's no gentleman! He says he'll do everything he can to block us, and that I needn't think he'll pull his punches on a woman. And he says that the day we bring our first stage down from High Town, we can expect real trouble from Kip Matson."

Grif chuckled. "An honest-to-god *hombre*, eh? You know, Katie, he reminds me of a young bull just dying to try his horns. But sometime he's going to run into an old mossy-horn that's already learned to use his. And that might just be me."

Then Katie said in a whisper: "Do you know something, Grif . . . he . . . he *chews!*"

"I'd be amazed if that's the worst thing he does."

"It's too bad, too. He might be nice, if he weren't so belligerent and didn't have such nasty habits."

Grif smoked a last pipe at his window, clad in underwear and boots. He thought of Annie, a thousand miles away in Wyoming. He thought of what he had told her. "You give me a year, and I'll be back with a satchelful of double eagles and a goin' ranch!"

But tonight he was feeling the uncertainty of a man who has just one talent and knows the demand for that talent is failing. For Grif belonged to the stage days, and practically everywhere except in this little pocket of the mountains those days belonged to cracked-voiced old-timers on hotel porches. That was why it was a damned shame that Matson couldn't see what Grif could: that there were enough guns leveled against the Concords without the men who ran them getting into squabbles.

Grif was down at the bank when it opened. The two tellers were still bringing trays of coins to their cages. A big, loosely built man was talking to the bank manager. Grif finished opening a checking account and went back to where they were talking. He introduced himself to the manager, whose name was Grant. Grant indicated the other man.

"Joe Porter," he said. "What can I do for you?"

"I'm looking for workmen," Grif told him. "Maybe you can tell me just where to start."

"If it's workmen," said Grant, "Joe, here, is your man. Joe's head of the grange. Guess you've got a few boys ready to turn a dollar, haven't you?"

Porter took a cigar out of his mouth. He was about Grif's age, built in the heavy architecture of a man who has spent his life hammering a living out of the soil, but wearing the marks, now, of one who has finally learned how to make the soil work for him. He wore a good black suit and a string tie; his fingers were work-thickened. On one hand he wore a big gold ring set with a ruby. What hair he had left was almost white, but his eyebrows were still black, giving him a ferocious look.

"What kind of workmen you looking for?" he asked.

Grif hedged. "Oh, sort of general work. I need a couple of boys that are good with horses, and maybe a dozen others."

"You might go down to the Grange Hall," Porter suggested. "You'll find a few, at least. After yesterday's flood there may be some more."

Grif thanked him, and stood on the walk looking for the Grange Hall. He discovered it downstreet, a two-story brick building that looked like a firehouse, half hidden by trees. When he reached it, he saw a long shady porch populated by eight or ten men in chairs tilted against the wall. They were occupied with the immemorial pastimes of the laborer between engagements—checkers and gossip. Action froze when Grif started up the board sidewalk through the rustling Lombardy poplars.

Grif looked them over. "Well, sir," he said pleasantly. "It looks like I've come to the right place. I need men that ain't afraid of work. I've got some money I'm either going to drink up or pay out in wages. How many of you boys would like a piece of it?"

A lean, red-headed man with a lanky nose and eyes like a St. Bernard's spoke. "What kind of pay, mister?"

"Ninety a month. You board yourselves."

There was a rustle of interest that made chair legs scrape on the bricks. "Steady?" the redhead asked.

"Twelve months out of the year! There's no off-season in my business."

"What *is* your business, mister?"

Grif hitched up his belt. He met the questioning eyes. "Stagin'. I'm hiring for the Mountain Stage Line."

They all sat back, while mouths tightened and eyes took their measure of him. The man with the red hair began to shake his head. "I guess not," he said. "We sort of like our standing in this town."

Grif knew men. He was able to see, through the quick distrust of their faces, a sort of hunger in them, a need to be doing something useful, to be carrying a pocketful of silver dollars home to their families Saturday night. And he went after this weakness like a good boxer.

"Standing?" he said, and he smiled. "It looks to me, boys, like you're doing more setting than standing. What do they pay you for whittling on them sticks and getting a man into the king's row? That's what I thought! Well, sir, there may be some prejudice against my outfit because it caters to the hydraulics. I'm new here, and I don't know about the ins and outs of that. All I know is I invested in this thing blind, and I'm going to have my money out of it. First thing I'm going to do, when I get to operating, is to apply for extension of my franchise, so that I can by-pass this here High Town if I want. But right now I'm asking for men. How many are signing on?"

Right then he could pick the ones that were his and the ones who stood pat on their suspicion, and the redhead was one of the latter. "Even if we wanted to," he declared, "Joe Porter would read us right out of the grange. It's no dice, mister."

"It looks like good sense to me," Grif commented, "to take what comes along, grange or no grange."

Then they heard a man striding down the walk beyond the trees. Everyone looked up when he turned in. It was the man Grif had met in the bank, the man called Joe Porter. He came to stand a foot from Grif and stared at him with blunt hostility.

"The teller says you opened an account for Mountain Stage Line," he said tartly. "That being the case, I'll recommend you to the street, right quick."

"Let's leave that up to the boys," Grif suggested. "If you

really want to know what I plan to do, I'll draw you a blue-print over a couple of beers."

"All I want from you is to see you hightail it out of here," snapped Porter. "Andy," he said, glancing at the redhead from under those still black brows, "I'm going to want an explanation of this. I thought you were grange men. . . ."

Andy said hastily: "I was just telling him, Joe, that. . . ."

Grif interrupted. "You can scratch this windbag's back after I leave. Anybody here got the guts to go to work for me? I'll make it a hundred."

Porter let him turn to face the men. Then he brought the edge of his hand like a blunt axe against Grif's neck. For a moment Grif was blind. He fell against the railing. He went over it like a plank and landed in the weeds beneath the porch.

Up on the porch the grangers were howling with laughter. The redhead was doubled over, pointing at him; another man had fallen back on a chair to laugh in a high voice like a woman's, and Porter stood in the midst of them with a contemptuous smile on his face, watching Grif get up.

Grif's head was clearing. He was wild with pain and the shame of being taken off guard. He threw off his black box coat, let his old Dragoon pistol, slung under his arm, drop with it, and started up the stairs.

The laughter stopped. Porter was at the head of the steps, but he was not alone. Andy was with him, and two other men. But Grif kept right on.

III

The one called Andy fancied himself a fighter. "Leave me have him, Joe!" he said. He stepped in front of the others and struck a bare-fist stance, his left arm straight out, the knuckles turned under. He looked to Grif about as dangerous as a monkey on a stick, and he went into him accordingly.

Andy stabbed at his head, but Grif smashed the blow aside and carried him back with a fist to the jaw. The redhead's fancy defense blew up. He tried to wrestle, kick with his knee, and choke. Grif had been handling his kind for years. He tagged him once more on the chin, hard, caught his loosening body, and threw him off the porch.

Porter moved in, two of the others with him. Grif swung and missed, then swung and connected and felt a sharp pain on his ear as he took a wild swing of Porter's. Porter fought slowly and heavily, dangerous only because there was real power when he hit. But he had the others, and they were beginning to crowd Grif back down with a haymaker. It sent him over backward, to sprawl on his back. A man left the porch feet first, yelling.

Grif could see the flat soles of his boots. He rolled, and, when the man landed, he was after him savagely, letting the whole tide of his hatred loose on him. He mashed his nose and cut his eye. He was choking him with both hands when the others swarmed over him. It didn't take long after that. But when they finished, Grif was only one of four who lay on the ground. The faces of the walking wounded, too, looked as though it hadn't been much fun.

He awoke with the warm animal odors of a stable in his nostrils. He lay on a ticking of hay in a stall. When he sat up, he was green with nausea and his head rang like a church bell. His coat and gun lay near him, and Grif uncorked the canteen in the butt of the Dragoon pistol, with its walnut shoulder stock, and drank with his eyes closed.

A man came out of the harness room to stand there with a

headstall in one hand and an awl in the other. "Trough's outside, if you want to wash up."

Grif went out, touching each post as he went by. He took off his shirt and soaked his head, let the sun-warmed, mossy water stream down over his chest and belly.

Then the stableman watched him get into shirt and coat. "Two things you ought to remember," he declared. "Walk soft in a strange town, and don't try to steal another man's workmen."

"One thing you can remember," stated Grif, "is to keep your mouth shut until I ask you to open it."

"OK, OK! But it's still good advice. Joe Porter throws too much weight around here to be fooled with. He owns six farms . . . hires up to a hundred men in the harvest season. Joe's a damned good man," he added loyally.

"He'll have his chance to prove it one of these days." Then Grif asked: "Where is the Mountain Stage stock kept?"

"Here. I've got 'em out to pasture. Wild as mountain sheep! Any time you want to pay the bill, you can have them. The stages are in the livery barn."

"I'll have the money in the morning. I want a stage ready to move at nine o'clock. I don't care if the horses are drinking whisky and chewing tobacco, I want 'em hitched."

He told Katie she might as well spend the next day or two opening the house on North Street. "I'll hire a crew in High Town," he said. "Should have had sense enough to start there in the first place."

It was the rawest stage team Grif had ever seen that he inspected the next morning. Meadow grass puts nothing much in a horse but vinegar and stomp, and these animals had lived on Bluestem for eight months. Four hostlers had to keep them in check as Grif climbed up to take the ribbons.

Curious faces were turned toward the stables all along the street, but no crowd had gathered because in theory a Mountain stage wasn't even worth watching while it got wrecked. But when it started to move, windows went up and doors opened. A cannonball would have been no comparison, because artillery couldn't whinny. But for speed, Grif could have reached over and lighted his cigar on the fuse.

Most of Grif's driving had been down in Arizona, years ago, when there'd been a driver shot off the box, or he'd substituted for a sick one. But he knew which lines controlled which horses, except that in this case none of them controlled any of the brutes. They were out of town in thirty seconds and hitting the road up the side of the mountain.

He let them run. The dusty old Concord walloped along, rocking on her bull-hide thorough braces. On the outside turns the iron tires kicked gravel over the cliffs. Grif's strategy came out when the horses, after the first explosion of energy, began to slow. He gave them the whip, then, not over their heads, but on their hides, and he stood up and bawled curses at them: "Run, you devils! Earn the grub you've been stealing out of my pockets!"

He kept them running until they began to stagger. Then he let them trot. He sent some messages up the ribbons and got responses. They would be stage horses by the time they ate hay in High Town.

The stage road kept climbing until the whole floor of Indian Valley lay spread out for inspection. When Grif looked at the acres blotched with yellow detritus from the mines, he wasn't surprised there was some bad feeling about Ed Broderick. But what damned the valley, in Grif's eyes, was that they jumped a man even before he knew what the set-up was. He had a self-righteous desire to bring Porter and Matson and all the rest of them to their knees before he was through.

The chain of hills that bound the basin on the south began to curve to meet the mountains the stage road followed. Grif came around an elbow of the hills and saw, a few miles ahead, a blue notch where the two chains merged. Nearer, he saw smoke, a flash of white water, and the shine of new lumber, and knew High Town was coming up.

He didn't need to ask how the town got its name. Its main street lay like a string along the side of the mountain. It had the impermanent look of so many of the Mother Lode towns, as though they had just sat down to rest before hurrying on to the next bonanza. There was hardly enough level ground to build on. The buildings on the right side of the street, as he entered, were shored up at the rear to keep them from sliding down into the cañon. Grif drove slowly through town, counting one hotel, nine saloons, and no churches. At the far end he found his objective: a small, slab-sized shack fronting for a string of lodge-pole corrals on the hillside. Across the front of it was the title of the **Mountain Stage Company.**

He unharnessed the team, turning it into a corral. He had three things to do; the first was to eat. Afterward, he ordered hay for the animals. Last, he found a printing shop and got a sign made in large block print. He selected the largest bar in town.

"Five dollars, brother," he told the owner, "if you'll let me use a back table for an office this afternoon."

The saloonkeeper read the sign: **Bonus Pay for Stage Jobs! Inquire Within!** "Why not?" he said.

Grif posted the sign, bought three quarts of bourbon, and sat down to wait. In ten minutes, his first customer appeared. He was a young fellow with a Roman nose and dark sideburns and a look of casual confidence. He dropped his Stetson on the seat of a chair and turned another to straddle the back of it.

"What's the game, pardner?"

Grif poured him a drink. "I pay a hundred a month for stable and office hands, two hundred for shotgun guards, and three-fifty for drivers. I've got cash to pay, and I go to work as soon as I can get a crew."

"You'll operate between Indian Valley and High Town?"

"Every day in the year."

The other accepted a drink. "This'll want some thinking about," he stated. "Keep one of those driving jobs open for about an hour. I'll be back. Name's Heydenfeldt," he added.

Grif liked the easy swing of his walk, the big lazy cut of him. Cocky, perhaps, but the kind he needed to open a stage line in this country.

Before Heydenfeldt returned, Grif signed on two hostlers and a Mexican to tend stock at the Strawberry Cañon station. Then Heydenfeldt was back with a man who didn't come above his chin, but to whom every man in the room spoke as he passed through. As they approached the table, Grif saw that he carried his poster in his hand, torn down the middle as though it had been ripped off the wall. Grif held his drink in one hand and made no effort to get up.

Heydenfeldt said: "This is the guy I was telling you about, Ed. Holbrook, meet Ed Broderick."

They looked at each other, but neither man acknowledged the introduction. Then Broderick tossed the torn poster on the table. "There's an easier way than this to get things done in High Town, Holbrook. Ask for Ed Broderick."

Grif said: "I sort of muddle along, but I generally get things done without asking for anybody."

Heyenfeldt's eyes took the affront darkly, but Broderick grinned and sat down. "So do I," he chuckled. "But look how much better you could do if you did take the easy way once in a while." And he handed Grif a sheet of letter paper and a list of fifteen or twenty names.

"Stage hands. It's all I could raise in a half hour, but I can get all you want."

"What's it going to cost me?"

Broderick signaled a bartender. "A drink . . . on me."

The barman brought straight whisky. Grif looked Ed Broderick over critically. He was dark, with a heavy, under-shot jaw and white teeth. His shirt collar was undone, show-ing a strong brown neck. Broderick and Heydenfeldt raised their drinks and waited for Grif, but Grif let his sit before him. Broderick asked: "Not drinking?"

Grif said: "Not until I know the man who's buying. All I know about you is that a flood of your damned slickers almost drowned me day before yesterday. And that don't make me thirsty enough to drink with you."

Both men set down their drinks, but it was Heydenfeldt who slowly stood up. His chair toppled; all over the saloon, men turned quickly.

IV

Broderick lifted a pudgy brown hand. "Len!" Heydenfeldt stood there, staring down at Grif. The whole focus of his tension was upon the bone-handled Colt at his side. Grif began to grin. He had seen killers before, but this man wasn't one; he was just an ambitious amateur.

"Show me how you killed Billy the Kid," he suggested.

Heydenfeldt didn't like the joke, but Broderick said impa-tiently: "Sit down. I can understand," he told Grif, "why you might be upset about hydraulic mining. But what would you say if I told you it wasn't my fault the river runs muddy?"

"I'd say, prove it."

Broderick stood. "Fine! We'll go downstairs and see just what happens when you start up the Long Toms."

There was a crudely backed road that bent itself back and forth down the timbered cañon-side. They walked down it in deep red dust, the sun brilliant in the areas between patches of shade thrown by blue oak and digger pine. Upcañon, Grif could see a small log dam with a wooden flume walking on wooden stilts toward the diggings.

The road came out above the workings. On the near side the flume, now dry, brought water to a wooden bulkhead, from which a fat iron pipe conveyed the water to a distributor. At the distributor, the immense pressure of it was deployed into three smaller pipes ending in the great eight-inch nozzles called monitors. Across the slot-like cañon, the jets from these nozzles had cut away the hill to bare bones.

Broderick spoke to a workman nearby. "Cut 'm on." They walked down to the platform from which the monitors were operated. Broderick took the big counterbalanced tiller in his hand.

The water came foaming down the wooden trough. Grif could hear it boiling inside the bulkhead, crowding through the pipe into the distributor. Then the monitors came alive. Water leaped across the cañon in two shouting torrents, hurling itself against the far bank, cutting out boulders the size of a hogshead, pulling the higher earth down and flushing it with the rest on down to the sluices. Broderick played the giant's spout back and forth, throwing those tons of water where he wanted them, and the earth came down, and the brush, and stones to crush a stagecoach. Then he gave the signal to cut the water off.

He was smiling when he turned to Grif, a small man flushed with power. "That's how she's done. The slickens go over the blocks in the sluices, and we settle out the color with mercury. The rest goes down to Indian Valley. You know why?" Accusation came into his voice. "Because a pack of shiftless hoe-men haven't the get-up to maintain a débris basin! I've offered to pay for the materials, just to shut them up. It's no dice. The state says they're to put up débris basins to protect their crops, but they'd rather go broke grumbling."

Heydenfeldt's sullen, dark face was turned toward the yellow flood brawling downcañon. "Tell him the rest," he said.

Broderick gave him an impatient glance. "Why bring personalities into it? Well, you might as well know," he growled to Grif. "Somebody thinks I've got a nice thing here. He'd like to see me run out, and take over himself. I think I could pacify these farmers, except that he keeps them stirred up."

"Joe Porter?" asked Grif bluntly.

Broderick shrugged. "We'll talk about it someday. So, now," he said, "you know who you'd be drinking with. The bottle's still up there."

Grif tried to look into him, through his straightforward brown eyes. He liked the way Broderick talked; he liked his openness. Finally he put out his hand. "Let's have a drink," he said.

Broderick was right. In High Town, it was Ed Broderick who got things done. Daily transportation to Indian Valley was something he could get enthusiastic about. He brought horse-breakers from nearby ranches to bring the stock back into shape. He had the corrals repaired, the stage cleaned up and greased.

Heydenfeldt had driven for Jim Birch in the old bonanza days. Grif was glad to have him on the box the morning the hostlers backed the team into the breeching for the first run. At ten o'clock, Ed Broderick came down to the stage station with a strongbox, heavy with bullion consigned to Wells

Fargo, in Indian Valley, for reshipment to the mint. He had a
light gray Stetson on this morning, and a pin-striped suit. He
wasn't going to miss the inaugural trip.

Grif was coming from the office when the tin voice of a
stage horn echoed back and forth across the cañon. From the
head of town came the high thunder of hoofs, and then Kip
Matson and his guard, riding the box of a Sierra stage,
whirled down the street. The stage didn't even slow down. It
went by as though High Town didn't exist.

Heydenfeldt released a yell and started climbing to the
box. "Let's go!" he shouted. "If we can't beat Matson, we
ought to be trundlin' a wheelbarrow!"

Everything snapped to business. The horses lunged
against the breast straps, the chains swung, and iron tires
ground a path into the soft, fresh dust. They hadn't gone a
quarter of a mile when Matson looked back. Then the Sierra
stage's wheels spun a little more frantically, and the red dust
whipped higher behind it.

Heydenfeldt drove with hard, stubborn determination,
sitting back against the horsehair with his feet braced widely
and the ribbons held just so. His whip was never still.

They entered Strawberry Cañon, which wound through
the hills before coming out on the hairpin Johnson Grade
down to the valley. Heydenfeldt's leaders were coming
abreast of the Sierra's rear boot when Matson's relay station
came into view. Grif watched to see what he would do. If he
put the pressure on his animals, they might hold out until
they hit the Johnson Grade. The man who was in the lead
here had the race locked in his strongbox, because there was
no pausing for eight miles.

Suddenly Matson pulled out of the road and rattled into
the station yard. Grif grunted. It took guts to do that. But, after all, a stage man's first duty was to his horses. It was no par-

ticular glory to Matson, he figured.

Heydenfeldt thumbed his nose as they rolled by.

He kept them running hard until they reached Grif's relay station, a mile farther on. Here he swung in, yelling for the hostlers. While the hostlers changed teams, he stood by with one foot on a hub, commenting on their fumbling with vigorous profanity. Just as the chains were latched, the warm, still air brought them the sound of Matson's stage coming down the road.

The stationkeeper sprang back, waved, and watched the Concord wheel into the road. Heydenfeldt held the ribbons in one hand and began to use the whip. Grif's fists clenched, but he kept still. Matson's stage came pounding up. Grif looked across at Matson, just a few feet away. His hat was off; the wind filled his blue Army shirt. Grif could see the bulge of a chunk of Navy tobacco in his cheek.

Very soon it settled into a hang-and-rattle run for the Johnson Grade. Matson would pull ahead a couple of rods, and then Heydenfeldt's whip would talk a little more speed out of his horses and the positions would be reversed.

Suddenly the cañon opened up. The grade was ahead. Len Heydenfeldt stood up, and Grif saw Matson lean forward and talk to his team like a jockey. They were on a stony ridge that curved away to the right and ran against a hill, and here the road narrowed down to a bare wagon track.

Matson was suddenly pulling ahead, foot by foot. Right then Grif knew that the rival driver had outgeneraled his own. He had a tough, veteran team before him, but he hadn't let them stretch. That last ounce of fight he had saved for the finish, and now his horses were walking away, and nothing but the loss of a wheel could stop them.

Heydenfeldt chewed his lip. Suddenly his hands twisted, and the team lunged sharply against Matson's. Confused, the horses swerved and stumbled into the ditch. The stage went with them, Matson standing up and shouting at the horses. Then, desperately, he swung about to lash at the other driver. But it was too late, too late for anything but picking a soft spot and jumping.

The last thing Grif saw was the team going down and the stage overturning among the great gray stones.

V

Finally he could breathe again. Finally he could seize Heydenfeldt's wrist and shout in his face: "Pull them in, you damned fool! You may have killed somebody back there. What were you trying to do?"

Heydenfeldt handed in the lines, and his long leg stretched on the brake. He looked back. Grif saw dazed passengers crawling out of the Concord. He saw Matson and his shotgun guard on their knees among the boulders. The horses were threshing wildly in a tangle of harness.

"Nobody hurt," Heydenfeldt decided glibly. He kicked off the brake, and they started down the grade. "They'll get her going some way or other. If we went back now, there'd be gunsmoke. Let 'em cool off. Then they'll realize it might have been an accident."

Grif stared at him. "*Was* it an accident?"

Heydenfeldt's mouth grinned. "Mebbe."

"Only it wasn't. You may have been Jim Birch's top whip, but you're through with the Mountain Line when we finish the run. That was a sneak punch."

Heydenfeldt shrugged. "You want to run a stage line, don't you? Well, you won't make out long as a member of the Purity League. But suit yourself."

When they reached the home station, Grif said: "You can come inside and draw your time."

Katie was there to greet him, all rosy with the excitement of seeing her first stage pull in. "Isn't it wonderful, Grif! We're operating!"

"I hope we can still say that tomorrow," Grif growled.

He got a sack of silver from the safe, but as he was counting it, Ed Broderick came in. Broderick was chewing his cigar; he looked mildly amused. "Len tells me you don't like his driving." He chuckled.

"I don't give a damn for any man who wins races that way."

Broderick struck him playfully on the shoulder. "It ain't as serious as all that, Grif. The kid's wild, not mean. I'll lay down the law to him."

"I already did. He's washed up, with me."

Katie Gillison came in. Broderick's eyes took in the clean, feminine lines of her, but his gaze was absent. "That's too bad. I'm kind of proud of my boys. I don't think I'd let one get fired without taking the whole crew off."

Grif looked up sharply. So it was that way! Broderick could be open-handed, but he tied a little cord to every gift he made. And Grif knew he had him in a corner, because without men he had no stage line. He dumped the silver dollars into the sack and drew the cord.

"I can't match an argument like that," he admitted. "But the next time he slips, I'll horsewhip him all the way down the grade."

Grif and Katie had an early dinner, returning at dusk to do the bookkeeping on this first run. Figures fretted Grif. He let Katie take over, strolling to the door to watch the sunset sift its glory over the valley below the town. Leaning lazily against the door, he saw Matson's stagecoach come reeling down the street.

The smooth poplar sheering was splintered. The nigh door was lashed on with rope, and it was rope, too, which kept the tongue in one piece.

Katie came to stare. "What in heaven's name! Grif, there's been a wreck!"

Grif hitched up his pants. "Honey, it might be a good idea if you ran down to the hotel for a while. There's liable to be another collision, right here in this office. That's why I tried to fire Heydenfeldt. He forced Matson off the road at the top of the Johnson Grade."

Katie appeared startled; then she declared: "If there was any trouble, I'm willing to bet Matson started it."

"Not this time. This one is on us. I can talk to Matson better if I have a free hand."

Katie returned to the desk. "Just the same, I'm going to be right here when he comes. Whatever may have happened, he asked for it."

She pulled down the ceiling lamp on its chain and lighted it. In fifteen minutes Kip Matson, with Joe Porter beside him, strode into the office of the Mountain Stage Line. One side of Matson's face was ribbed with deep scratches, and there was still red earth ground into his clothes, but he looked angry and vigorous enough for two men.

"We played your game today, Holbrook," he declared. "We'll play mine tonight."

"And when he gets through with you," Porter stated, "we're going to try you in court for attempted manslaughter, if there's anything left to try."

Katie was confronting the men with her pen tucked in her hair and her arms crossed. She could put a fine irony into her voice. "This is about how I thought you'd fight, Mister

Matson. When you found you couldn't beat us legitimately, you'd want to use your fists. Maybe you'd rather fight me, instead of Grif. Or are you afraid I'd scratch?"

Matson's grin was sardonic. "You're a scratcher if I ever saw one! But my quarrel's with Holbrook. And if he ain't yellow as butter, he'll come down to Grogan's Alley with me."

"Son," Grif said, "you've got a grievance, but that wreck was Heydenfeldt's fault. Have the stage fixed and send me the bill."

"I'll take it out in hide. You've made trouble ever since you hit town. I don't put it down to your credit that you take a woman as pardner, either, to hide behind her skirts."

Grif's shoulders moved. "If you're really looking for a scrap," he said slowly, "I think that's about the angle to use. Try it again."

He was ready to swing, that was in the set of his feet and shoulders, but Porter, with his black brows bristling and his thin hair still rumpled from the wreck, grunted: "You'll get your fight, Holbrook, but take my advice and don't start anything here. I reckon the boys in town would just about tear you to rags if they found an excuse."

Grif took off his coat. "Grogan's Alley is jake with me."

They started out the door into the late dusk, but Katie had one more shot to fire at Matson. There was temper in this quiet, blue-eyed girl, and it had been stirred. "You're nothing but a . . . a tobacco-chewing ruffian!" she flared. "I'll bet you can't even beat Grif with your fists, and you fifteen years younger!"

Matson stopped, and he was laughing. Some of the hard pucker of his eyes fled from that smile; he looked what he was, then—a man not long out of his teens, hiding behind a manufactured toughness.

"I'll bet a kiss I can!" he said. "And I'll hold the stakes."

He took a bear-hug kiss from Katie before she tore away and began to strike at him. Agilely he dodged her. As he and the others started down the boardwalk, his laughter boomed back out of the shadows.

Grogan's Alley was fifteen feet of unsanctified earth separating the National Hotel and the Kitty-Bar-the-Door Saloon. Out here, where the smell of sage was strong and the pines stood like dark pickets only a few hundred yards beyond, they stopped.

Porter bent, grunting, to pick up a scantling. "Just in case you try to pull a belly gun, Holbrook," he remarked with frosty humor.

Grif knew how Porter fought, and he didn't like the set-up. But it was too late to bring his own second, now, with Matson already squaring away to him.

Matson came in with a rush. Grif blocked him, planted his palm in his face, and shoved him away. Matson bounced back. This time he found Grif's ear with a roundhouse blow. Grif went after him with anger fuming in his head. He was heavier than the other man, but an inch or two shorter. Older and slower, maybe, but as tough as only the stage trails, with their slow fires of heat and cold and peril, can make a man.

It was a good fight. Matson's style was a stinging attack, a headlong cavalry charge that slowed only when he was knocked back. Grif fought like a grizzly, mauling, wrestling when he could, slugging. They would be after each other furiously for a minute or two, and then, with both men exhausted, the battle would ebb.

Grif was finding that this lanky youngster could take punishment as well as give it. And he was finding something else: that his own legs were giving out. He could stand Matson off, but he couldn't go in with the bounce he needed to wear him down. Matson didn't let Grif rest; he was after him like a hornet every second.

So, in the end, Grif knew it would have to be his Sunday punch. An ox couldn't stand up to that swing, which started out in the barn and ended with smoke leaking out of his knuckles. It was like a Forty-Five slug. Anywhere it hit a man, it would knock him down.

Matson seemed to be maneuvering for a haymaker, too. Grif shoved his jaw out a little farther and swung. He felt a glorious pain in his fist. Matson was down, rolling over in the weeds. The punch had hit him high on the forehead, but it had done the job.

Grif took a deep breath—and saw Matson dragging himself to his knees. He saw him stagger out on the road and sway. Then he forgot the stage man, as Porter bawled almost in his ear. "Drop it, you fool! Drop it, or. . . ."

Porter lunged past Grif, and the scantling whistled. Matson went down again, with a slow, bewildered amazement on his face. Porter bent and picked something up out of the dust, and for a long time he stood with his head bent, staring at it. Grif moved forward. It was a belly gun, a double-barreled Derringer, which the granger held.

Porter's eyes raised. "I'll be damned," he muttered. "I . . . will . . . be . . . damned! I'd known Kip ten years, but you never really know a man till you see him in a fight."

VI

They stood there in the warm night. Far up in the hills, coyotes yipped. There were sounds from town, the dry scratching of weeds as the wind brushed them. More than surprise, Grif felt sharp disappointment.

Porter sighed and shoved his hands in his pockets. "I'm

sorry, Holbrook," he said. "Sorry all around. I wish to hell he'd whipped you honestly, because you needed it. But I guess you know what this means. You can go to the sheriff and prefer charges against him."

"To hell with that," Grif grunted. "His own conscience ought to punish him enough. That, and not being able to face me on the street." He took out a handkerchief and dabbed a cut lip, and started up the road. Porter called after him.

"I suppose you're going to talk this all over town?"

"Not if he keeps in line. If he doesn't, there's no telling what I may do. But you can tell him this . . . Grif Holbrook's playing for keeps."

In the office, he poured himself a half tumbler of whisky from the bottle he kept in his desk. He slouched in the swivel chair. If it weren't for Annie, he would be willing to sell his stock and quit right now. Everything was out of joint. As far as he could tell, everybody around here had a knife in somebody else's ribs.

He sat there for half an hour before Katie came in from the back. She had been sleeping here until she could get the house on North Street cleaned up. She wore a soft gray dressing robe and her hair was up in papers. She set her candle down.

"Good heavens!" she exclaimed. "Is that how a winner looks, or a loser?"

"It's all in your point of view," Grif observed. "But I was the one that walked off."

"Did you hurt him badly?" Katie tried to sound off-handed, but her eyes betrayed her.

"You can't hurt them when they're as young and tough as he is. Only their looks, and he didn't have much to lose."

He started to leave, but at the door he stopped, because Kip Matson, white-faced and bloody, was standing on the walk looking at him. Involuntarily he moved back, reaching for his gun, but Matson merely came up the two steps and stood with his hands hanging down the seams of his pants. He had no gun.

"Did you tell her?" he asked.

Grif said slowly: "You lost, son. Just forget how. There's two sides to every street, and it'll be best if you and I keep the ruts between us."

Matson spoke to Katie. "I pulled a gun on him, and Joe Porter crowned me. Did he tell you?"

Katie stared at him and did not reply. Matson turned. "You don't have to keep frettin' that gun, Holbrook. I came here to tell you something, and you can take it or leave it. I didn't pull my gun on you. The gun Porter showed me I never saw before."

Grif spoke shortly. "I saw him pick it up from your feet after he hit you. That was good enough for me."

"It's not good enough for me, because I wasn't carrying one. I told Porter so, and he said maybe somebody framed me. He claims he saw it under my belt when I crawled out of the weeds, and said I was reaching for it." He shook his head. "I don't know whether he's lying to me or . . . or what."

Grif handed him the bottle. "What you need is a drink. Then get out."

Matson, without tasting the liquor, put it down. He scowled. He was trying to pull his mental shoulders back, to look hard and self-sufficient, but bewilderment stood in his eyes. "I said you could take it or leave it," he declared. "But I'm telling you this . . . somebody framed me, and if I find out who . . . well, I'll be carrying a gun for a few days, until I find him."

Grif turned his back and picked up some papers from the desk. "Don't bang the door when you leave," he said.

Matson did.

Katie's voice was almost lost in the room. "Do you . . . really think he was framed, Grif?"

"I don't know. I saw the gun at his feet when Porter stooped over him. That's all I know. That, and that I need some sleep."

For the next two weeks, Indian Valley's rival stage lines ran their own ways in peace. Grif came in from a run one day to find a message from Porter, two short lines in a sealed envelope. **Will you visit me at my place, today? I have news which might interest you.**

Grif rented a horse, after debating it, and started for Porter's farm. As he rode, he thought about Porter for the first time since the fight. He couldn't quite swallow Porter's change of heart. A man didn't sandbag a friend to help an enemy, unless, perhaps, he was trying to keep his friend from a hang noose.

He branched from the stage road down a side road he identified by Porter's mailbox. Shimmering green-and-silver madroña trees lined the road. The fields beyond were cut transversely with rows of rich green truck on the moist red-bronze earth. There was gold in those fields, just as surely as there was gold in Broderick's diggings. It was incredible, to Grif, that the farmers would not take the trouble to protect their crops with a silt basin.

Porter had his impressive, two-storied home in a grove of locusts and elms. He stood at the top of the steps as Grif tied his horse.

Porter wore a frowning gravity as they went into an office. The granger offered cigars, but he didn't light his; he sat in an armchair rolling it between his palms. Then he got up and took a folded paper from his desk and sat down again. He appeared disturbed.

"I suppose," he growled, "you've got as much right to this as anybody. I've spent two weeks trying to decide, ever since the scrap that night. Look it over."

Grif glanced at it. About all he could deduce was that somebody named J. Henry Biggs had been awarded a judgment against the Sierra Stage Company of Indian Valley.

Porter lighted his cigar. "It's a judgment against Kip Matson's outfit for injuries suffered by a passenger in a wreck four years ago. That was before Matson bought the line, but he's responsible. It's for three thousand dollars. I don't imagine Kip could raise two on short notice."

"What are you doing with it?"

"My lawyer ran across it by accident. The case came up in Sacramento, where the man lived. He won by default. Kip's forgotten it by now. The old-timer got the judgment, but he was old and sick and didn't have the money to try to collect. I got it from him for three hundred." He looked at Grif from under those ink-black brows of his. "You've got to be realistic, Holbrook, even where friends are concerned. I trust Kip as much as I trust any man, but just in case he got to fraternizing with the wrong people. . . ."

You could look into his eyes, thought Grif, and see no deeper than the iris. "So where do I come in?" he asked. "What did I ride out here for?"

Porter made a roll out of the document. "I'll sell it to you for just what it cost me. You see how it would look if I pressed it, don't you? I could get an injunction in a minute, close him up. So could you. All's fair in war, but if I were to do it, they'd call me a Shylock. The point is, Kip's getting a little big for his britches. The next thing, he'll be by-passing us and dealing with High Town. How about it?"

What Grif did didn't come under the heading of common

sense. Without a word to the granger, he reached for a pad of blank checks on the desk and dipped a pen. He wrote Porter a draft for three hundred dollars and blotted it.

Porter said uncomfortably, trying to sound hearty: "You're not making any mistake, Holbrook! It's dog eat dog, in these things. After the other night, I made up my mind Kip didn't deserve the break I was giving him."

"Porter," Grif said, "if you ever gave anybody a break, it must have been a compound fracture of the left hind leg. There's only one trick in your book. Get somebody to do your dirty work for you. That's how it was the day at the Grange Hall. That's what you're doing now. I'll keep this . . . just in case. Someday, when the sign's right, I'm going to make it up to you for a lot of things. In the meantime, I'm getting out. There's a smell in here I don't want to get into my clothes."

His last view of Porter was of the bovine stupefaction on the man's face as the door slammed.

VII

Grif stuck the judgment away and forgot about it. He didn't know whether he had bought it to keep Porter from having the satisfaction of using it, or to give him a club over Matson. But he knew he would never use it. It was something he had somehow been compelled to do.

Ed Broderick kept him busy. There was a shipment of bullion every week, payrolls, light freight, the boots were always crammed. The monitors ran intermittently, a run and then the clean-up, then a day or two of fumes from the concentrate mill while the amalgam was reduced to bar gold.

Grif and Katie were making money. If it kept on, Grif could send for Annie in six months. But always there was uncertainty, that feeling of being in a treetop with no sure foundation under him. They moved the business office up to Indian Valley to be near their trade, and it was here, one day, that Matson's stage stopped and Matson got out of the stage, just like a passenger, and then the stage rolled on.

He came in, his long chin first. He stood at the counter and scowled at them. "I'd like to come in and set down a minute, if it's all right," he stated.

"What's on your mind?" Grif demanded.

"Business."

"Then it will have to wait. I take the stage down in fifteen minutes."

Matson said: "All right. I'll buy a ticket. Maybe Miss Gillison will come along. We can talk on the way down."

Grif glanced at Katie, and Katie's brows went up. "It's probably a waste of time," she said archly, "but a fare is a fare."

Matson's dark skin burned darker, but he paid for his ticket and sat down to wait. When Heydenfeldt brought the stage around, Grif carried out the strongbox. He loaded it into the front boot.

Matson took out a plug of Navy as they started. He set his teeth into it, but something caused him to glance at Katie, and thereafter he took it out of his mouth and replaced it in his pocket. "Excuse me, ma'am," he said. "Well, to get down to brass tacks . . . I want to buy you out."

"Well, now, that's a coincidence!" Grif declared. "We were just about to make you an offer, too. What made you think we'd sell?"

"Everything," Matson said shortly. "You can't get rich operating a line as short as yours. Not if the mine ever closes . . . and it's going to, one of these days."

"In the meantime," said Grif, "we're paying the bills."

Again Matson's hand went to his tobacco, but quickly dropped away. "I was thinking of five thousand," he remarked, and watched the effect on them.

Grif smiled. "Cash?"

"Why . . . half cash, maybe. The rest on time, at twelve percent."

"I don't think we'd be interested, would we?" Grif asked Katie.

"We might sell him the office furniture for that," Katie said with a sparkle.

The stage pulled into the relay station. There was silence while the horses were changed, but when it moved out again, Matson cleared his throat. "I could sweeten it a little, but you'd have to give me time. I'll tell you frankly, Holbrook . . . I'm getting tired of this see-saw business. I don't like my stages being held up an hour behind one of yours, when the driver decides to rest his horses. I've got a mail franchise, too, and you can't look around when you're working for Uncle Sam."

Rocks and shrubs were flashing past the windows. Heydenfeldt wasn't resting the horses today, Grif reckoned. He turned again to Katie.

"I think we're satisfied with things just about as they are, aren't we?"

Katie nodded. "But thank you for considering us worthy of being bought out, Mister Matson."

Matson's temper boiled up. "Dang a stubborn outfit like. . . ." He snatched out his tobacco, took a chew, and turned to the window.

Dust blew in through the windows next to the cliff, and Grif rolled down the curtains. They were now boiling down the grade. Gradually it came to him that the stage was making almighty good time. He thrust his head out the window.

"Hand 'em in a shade!" he shouted. He waited for a moment, and then repeated it. Only the grind of the wheels on the road answered him. Suddenly he knew that there was nobody on the box. He knew it without being able to see the driver's place, for the horses were running with the lines slack.

He turned back. Matson's eyes had a pucker of alarm. "Can you climb?" Grif asked him.

Matson didn't need a blueprint. He pulled his coat off and reached for the latch of the inside door. Oddly the door seemed to swing toward him, so that his hand passed the latch and struck the panel. But it was not the door alone swinging. It was the whole stagecoach, rising on its outer wheels as the inner ones came off the ground. Grif felt Katie lurch against him, and he grabbed her with one arm and hooked the other about the window sill. The Concord was going over.

Out of the confused seconds of rolling and sliding, of having dirt pour in through the windows and hearing from far off the screaming of horses, came a splintering crash, and then quiet. Grif was on his back on the seat. He couldn't see the others for dust. Matson groaned.

"You all right?" Grif muttered.

"I've alive," Matson panted. And then, alarm striking into his voice: "Where's the girl?"

Grif had lost her, somewhere in the slide down the hill. They found her on the bottom of the coach, pale as tallow, a little crumpled heap of petticoats and torn clothing. Matson slid down by her.

"Miss Gillison! Katie!" he cried. He threw a wild look at Grif.

Grif went to work on a sprung door. "Let's get her out of here," he said, hiding his own concern behind gruffness.

They got a door open, and Grif climbed out, Matson lifting the girl and handing her up to him. The stage had come to rest against a giant fir on the hillside, some hundred and fifty feet below the road. Bits of harness, broken spokes, and other gear lay along the slope. Horses seemed to be all over the hill, rolling and kicking. Matson scrambled out to take Katie into his arms and start toward a green patch of myrtle fifty yards away, where they could hope to find water.

They had not taken ten paces when a shingle of granite stirred just ahead of them. They heard the shot from the road a moment later.

Dumbly they stared at each other. A second shot galvanized Grif. He dragged Matson behind the tree that had stopped the Concord's slide.

It was crowded back there. Matson laid the girl down, sweating. "First hold-up we've had in six months," he declared. "Wouldn't I pick a day like this to go unheeled!"

Only six feet from the tree, half buried in sand, lay the strongbox. Grif dragged it to him. "If they get it," he vowed, "it'll be the last thing they do get!"

He had his Dragoon pistol out, the butt snug against his coat. He watched for a glimpse of one of the highwaymen. Presently a dark head showed in a cleft of rocks. Grif's shot was high.

He heard Katie moan. Immediately Matson was bending over her, touching her cheek, speaking her name. Grif was too busy to listen to half the foolish questions Matson was asking her. He got bark in his face from a close one. He thrust his right shoulder out for a snap shot, and saw the gunman disappear.

It was shot for shot for a while. Grif was now sure that they had only one gunman to reckon with. He fell to wondering about Heydenfeldt. Had they roped him off the box? They'd done for him somehow, that was sure. Then this second man had been in the road, no doubt, to booger the horses into running over the edge.

A calculator in the back of his mind counted shots. When he had fired four times, he spoke to Matson. "There's an extra cylinder in my left coat pocket. Powder and shot flasks in the other. Load 'er up."

He could feel Matson fumbling in his pockets. "Funny!" Matson muttered. "There's a powder flask, all right, but no shot. . . ."

"My God!" Grif's fingers verified it. The shot had been lost in the wreck. They were up against rifle slugs, with nothing but blank cartridges. . . .

Then he heard Matson start to chuckle. "Save the last shot, pardner. This feller's going to assay higher dead than he ever did alive. Here's a treasure box full of bullion we can whittle into slugs like cheese!"

All Grif needed was the suggestion. At a time like this, even bar gold was not sacred. He shoved the box halfway around the tree and put a shot into the padlock. Then he dragged it back, and Matson hauled the lid open. Grif looked into it, and Matson looked in, and then their eyes locked.

In neat, dull-gray piles were stacked half a thousand iron washers.

VIII

Right then, Grif did not try to figure it out. All he knew was that you couldn't slice iron washers with a penknife. He had one shot left, and it had to do the job.

There was stillness for fifteen minutes. Suddenly Matson said—"Listen!"—and stared in the direction of a gully fifty feet away. Buck brush and manzanita cloaked it. Grif heard nothing. Then gravel rasped dryly. He didn't know, now, whether the gunman on the road was working down to take them from the side, or whether there was a second man in the gully. He tested by moving away from the tree a couple of feet. There was no response from the road.

He nodded at Matson, and they moved the still-dazed girl to the other side of the tree. Both of them knew what had to be done. For the first time between them there was something approaching understanding.

Matson's hand gripped his shoulder. "Good luck, old-timer!"

Grif advanced step by step across the bare slope, toward the gully. Against his ribs was the polished walnut stock of the gun. He waited a long interval in the buck brush, getting his breath and listening. Then he went forward at a run, to plunge feet first into the barranca.

He saw the narrow, boulder-clogged wash below, just about as he'd pictured it. But what amazed him was that the man who crouched on his knees there, gun slashing pale saffron fire up at him, was no strange dog of the stage trails. It was Len Heydenfeldt!

Grif's legs crumpled when he landed. He went down on his face, but his gun was out in front of him. He fired that last shot at Heydenfeldt. Without waiting for the effect, he reached for a stone to follow up with. But Heydenfeldt was done. He was crumpling on the sand with a hand against his breast. He would tool his horses down a dark trail tonight.

Grif disarmed him, made sure he was dead, and went back for Matson.

There were some ugly facets to it that Grif did not like. If Heydenfeldt had been pulling a hold-up, he would have thrown the treasure box out first. Murder had been in his heart. But why?

Matson seemed to be thinking mostly about the washers. "That bears out something I've been thinking for a long time," he said. "Miners have been poking around here for years, but nobody ever found enough gold to plate a horseshoe before Broderick came along. See what it stacks up to? He's using the mines as an excuse to run out the grangers. There isn't four-bits worth of gold up there! Lord knows what he expects to gain by it. You can see," he said, accusingly, "what kind of a four-flusher you've been playing up to."

Grif said gruffly: "I'll talk about it after I've talked to Broderick."

Katie recovered, except for a headache, after Matson had made her bathe her face and neck in the cold water of the creek. Then they caught three of the horses, got them up to the road, and started bareback for Indian Valley.

Grif did not waste time below. He rented a saddler and headed back up the grade. It was dark when he reached High Town. He asked after Broderick in the saloon, and the barkeeper reckoned he was still in his office down at the concentrate mill. Grif took the trail down the side of the mountain, passed the hydraulic diggings, and saw lights in the big sheet-metal structure leaning against the hillside.

In his office, Ed Broderick had charts spread out on a desk. His eyes went quickly over Grif's face. He smiled that quick, flashing grin. "No trouble, is there?" he asked.

"Heydenfeldt's dead," Grif declared. He straddled a chair and kept his glance on the mine boss.

"Dead!"

"With a slug right in his heart. One of my slugs. It was him or me. He sent the stage over the grade and opened up on us when we came out alive."

Broderick's grin vanished. He was sober as death. "I don't know whether you're joshing me or not," he said slowly.

"I'm wondering the same thing about you. Was it Heydenfeldt's idea, or did somebody tell him to do it?"

"Who would?"

"That's what I'm trying to decide. Maybe somebody who sends iron washers down every week, instead of gold."

Broderick took the surprise stolidly. He grunted. Then he got up and lit a cigar and stood at the window. In a moment he returned.

"Holbrook," he said, "a man shouldn't ever try to fool you. You're too noticin'. I might as well tell you about the mining set-up, because you'll find out anyway. But first I want this down in the book. Anything Heydenfeldt ever did was on his own hook. He was crazy as a jaybird. I only recommended him because he was a good driver. I'll admit he didn't like you any better than you did him. The way it looks to me, he was just pulling a hold-up."

Grif asked: "What about the mining?"

Broderick chewed the cigar, not looking at him. There were some lines in his face that Grif hadn't noticed before. He could read sourness and defeat there, but set against them was the hard thrust of his eyes—ruthless, fighting eyes—and the combination was not a nice thing to go against.

"I'll tell you a story," he said. "About a farmer who came from Ohio to California to make his fortune. He didn't have much money, not enough to buy forty acres of good Ohio land. Then he saw a railroad folder that said a farmer could make ten thousand a year in California, and not half try. But he found out that even out there a man without a stake was just a bum. He got angry finding that out.

"He run across a pack of other fellers having the same difficulty. He got them to help him in a scheme to set them all up on the best land they'd ever seen. He found one man with a little money to back them. Californians had put the hooks into these men, so why shouldn't they do the same for them? They bought up some used hydraulic equipment and took a mining claim up here. High Town wasn't much but a store and lot of road then.

"Well, Grif," he said, grinning and tucking his thumbs under his belt, "fifteen farmers have already folded, and I've bought up their land. We have to go easy, because we don't want to ruin the land completely. Just the crops, you see. Pretty soon about ten of us from High Town will change our addresses to Indian Valley."

"Joe Porter won't have to change his, will he?" Grif remarked.

Broderick smiled. "He's the one who had the money. He gets a third of the places we take over. Joe's doing all right. And, Grif, you can do all right for yourself, too, if you play it cagey."

"Talk about it," Grif suggested.

"We need a freight line as well as a stage line. This thing of yours is just a toy. After we move down the hill, we'll have tons of stuff to move every week. I may not be a miner, but give me some seed and a gang plow and I'll make this country over. Yes, sir! And you can be the stage and freight king of the Sierras, mister. And I'll back you to start."

He was striding back and forth. He was flushed, as he talked of something that he did not dare speak of to most men. He was a small man, physically, and like many such men he enjoyed power.

"It wants thinking about," said Grif. "But I always like to back a winner. I've got to size things up. If I like it, I'll be back."

Broderick said softly: "I'll give you twenty-four hours. But

I think you'll see my name written all over the valley, if you look close."

"I'll look," Grif agreed. "Suppose I'm interested . . . how long will I have to wait for some action?"

Broderick winked. "I've got a lot of water stored up. I look for something to happen in a week or two."

Grif had the feeling of being penned in a corner. At last he knew that Kip Matson was right. Broderick was playing blue-chip poker. The way it looked now, it was too late to cut his monitors off before they washed Indian Valley clean to Sacramento. All that build-up about the farmers being too lazy to build débris basins was hogwash. And Porter, with his double-barreled treachery, began to emerge as something more than a hypocrite.

Grif had a sense of urgency. Broderick was a long way ahead with his plans. But as long as he stayed in the game, he would play his cards close to his belly, and, when he stood up, it was with a straight, hard look at Broderick.

"I ain't promising a thing. But if it stacks up right, I'm with you. If it doesn't. . . ."

Broderick said: "I think it will, Grif. I sort of think it will."

IX

When Grif returned to Indian Valley the next day, Matson was with Katie at the stage office. He looked sheepish at being there, and Katie was as haughty as ever, but it was obvious to Grif that they were just hunting business to bring them together. And this morning he had some.

He told them about his conversation with Broderick, but he didn't kowtow any to Matson. "You can thank your own self for a lot of this," he declared. "If you didn't make it so pig-headed hard for anybody to co-operate with you, we might have had Broderick in the corner pocket by now."

"And if you hadn't aided and abetted him . . . !" Matson flared, but Katie cut in sharply.

"I should think there were enough people to fight without wrangling among ourselves."

They shut up. Presently Grif spoke. "You know these hoe-men better than I do. What would they do if we gave it to them, right on the line?"

"They'd lynch Porter and go after Broderick, and High Town would shoot the hell out of them . . . excuse me, ma'am. And we'd never be able to prove Broderick wasn't taking gold out of Deer Creek."

There was more silence, which Grif again broke. "What do you know about hydraulicking, Matson?"

Matson shrugged. "Not much. But I've seen how it's done."

"Know where we could get some equipment . . . pipe and monitors?"

"There's junk lying all over the hills. I could find you an outfit in two days."

"All right," Grif said, and his fingers began to drum. "We'll fight fire with fire. Pick out about a dozen men you can count on in a scrap, and hunt up some hydraulic equipment. I'm going to want it one of these days, real quick."

He told Matson what was in his mind. Matson was not enthusiastic, but when they split up, the younger man went down to his own place to get a wagon and go monitor hunting. Grif returned to High Town for his date with Ed Broderick.

He found him at the saloon. Broderick was having a beer with some of his men, but he called for a bottle and glasses, and they went to a table in back. "What's the good word?" he asked.

"I suppose I'm bein' a sucker," Grif said, "but I'll take cards. On one condition."

Broderick nodded, pleased. "What's that?"

"Well, the way I figure, a town needs a good fast road to a railhead if it's ever going to get out of knee-pants. By the stage road it's twenty-five miles to Auburn. I could build straight across the hills to the Central Pacific at Colfax, in less than twelve."

"For how much?"

"Say three thousand. Nothing fancy, just a freight road we can improve on as we go along. Another thousand or two for wagons and stock, and we'll have the fastest jerk-line outfit in California."

Broderick's fist struck the table. He liked to plan, to juggle figures, and move the pawns of empire like chess pieces. "You'll have a road crew tomorrow! I'll order the wagons in Frisco." He filled the glasses again and, raising his, smiled across it. "To the stage king of the Sierras!"

"To the boss hoe-man of Indian Valley!" Grif said.

He had his grading crew out in the morning. There was already a road running across the top of the log-and-earth dam, for the use of the men who tended the bulkhead regulating the flow of water to the distributors. Grif's plan was to bring the road across the dam and down the opposite side of the cañon from High Town. Here the cañon was so narrow a man could throw a silver dollar across it. Then the road would break south, toward the railroad.

He put men to work felling trees and grubbing out stumps. He organized another outfit with picks and shovels. "Main idea," he told them, "is to get a bar-pit dug alongside of where the road's gonna be. It won't be long till the rains, and I'm not wanting any of our work washed out."

Some of the men thought he was calling for too deep a ditch, but Grif was down the line every day, seeing that the pit measured a full four feet. He had the ditch about two-thirds of the way to the point across from High Town the day Kip Matson signaled him from the trees some distance up the hill. Grif found occasion to wander up that way.

Matson had two other men with him, one of them Engler, the shotgun messenger who had been on the box the day Grif arrived in Indian Valley. "How's she look?" Matson grinned.

Grif inspected the lengths of rusty pipe, the warped bulkhead and distributor. "I've seen purtier," he admitted. "How long will it take to set her up?"

"Ten, twelve hours, I reckon."

"Then you'd better camp up here where I can find you in a hurry. Broderick's going to turn the monitors on any day. When he does, it will be for the last time. And by the way . . . ," he said. He pulled the judgment he had bought from Porter out of his coat pocket. "You had better hang onto this thing or burn it up. If it falls into the wrong hands, it might cost you some money. I'm tired of having it around."

Matson was still staring at it when he walked away.

In two days the ditch was abreast of High Town, just a cow bawl across the cañon. That night Ed Broderick called Grif down to the mill office. Grif went in, stopping in the doorway to stare at Joe Porter. Porter stood by the desk. He gave Grif a broad wink and a foolish grin.

"I guess this is a little surprise to both of us," he said. "Didn't ever think I'd be working on the same side with you, Holbrook!"

"I guess it is," Grif said, and mustered a grin. He thought: *The things you have to do in this business!*

"This will be short and sweet," Broderick announced.

"Everything's set. Tomorrow at dawn, I cut the water on. Joe tells me there's a movement afoot to organize an Anti-Débris Association. We can't let this happen. I've given all my boys instructions to go heeled. If the hoe-men march up here and get hurt, it will be no skin off my nose . . . we're within our rights. But I don't think they'll have the spirit to march anywhere after the water hits 'em."

"What do you want me to do?" Grif asked.

"Just stand by. We'll leave everything to the monitors."

As he went out, Grif had the feeling that Broderick wouldn't have minded at all if he had saluted.

Darkness invaded the mountain town. Grif walked up to the dam and watched it from the trees. There was no guard. He crossed quickly and climbed to Matson's hide-out. The dozen men there had a small fire hidden in a cairn of rocks. They were smoking and drinking coffee when Grif arrived.

He gave them the news. "Broderick opens up his big guns tomorrow," he said. "We've got to have things set up by sunrise. Can you do it?"

"If they don't get wise to us," Matson said. He set the men to work in squads, carrying pipe and tools and lumber. He and Grif walked down to the ditch. Matson seemed to be trying to say something. Finally he grunted: "You had me under the stick with that paper. Did you know it?"

"Sure. So did Porter when he sold it to me. He was afraid it would spoil his own game if he used it."

"Why didn't you use it yourself?"

"Well, I've fought a lot of Indians in my time, but I never fought *like* one."

Matson said doubtfully: "I still don't get it."

They spent their small treasure of hours like misers. Matson took charge of the crew laying pipe. Grif's men cut

204

the ditch through to the dam, with only a small strip left to be torn out by black powder. In the gray hour before dawn, he followed the line right down to the muzzle. It was solid as stone. The Long Tom was set up directly across the cañon from where in the darkness they supposed Broderick's workings to be.

Then there was nothing to do but wait for dawn. Finally they could hear the sound of movement from the High Town side: men tramping down the trail and gruff voices firing orders. Dawn was burning along the mountains beyond the dam. Light mounted through the heavens, and down in the cañon stone and tree came out of nothingness.

Broderick could be seen with a gang of men sliding down the gravel bank to the monitors. They could hear him talking to someone.

Then they could hear Porter's voice rise sharply. *"Ed! What the hell is that?"*

Grif raised his arm high. Up at the dam a man bent hurriedly over a fuse. Broderick saw it all at a glance. He ran to the Long Tom, yelling at the men at the bulkhead. Some of the men with him began to scramble up the hill out of the way. It was plain that when the water began to roar a lot of earth was going to move—move mighty fast.

On the dam, Broderick's man threw a valve open, and water came foaming down the ditch. Grif kept waiting for the sound of the dynamite that would signify the opening of the ditch to his own monitor. Thirty seconds he waited, but nothing happened. Then from Broderick's monitor came a small jet of muddy water, which strengthened and lifted and tore a trench across the sandy cañon end as it felt for the men at the foot of the hill.

Grif saw the powder man raise his arms in a gesture of helplessness. He shot an order at Matson. "Get back in the rocks and wait!" It was a two-hundred-yard run uphill to the dam. He was burned out when he made it. The powder man stepped out to meet him.

"The damn' fuse won't burn!" he panted.

Grif bent at the fuse end. The last three feet of it were soaked; beyond that the cord appeared dry. He slashed at it with his knife and scratched a match on his boot. The fuse caught. He watched it a moment, until he was sure it was going.

He heard the granger yell: "Holbrook! Look out!"

When he looked up, Broderick's operator was running toward them from the bulkhead, a rifle in his hands. Grif brought his own gun up. "Lay 'er down!"

The man fired a wild shot without stopping to aim. It whipped the air above Grif's head. Grif's shot was studied. The man crumpled; he rolled in the dirt, and finally lay on his side, his legs pulling up.

Down the cañon Grif could see Broderick's monitor pouring its tons of water on the helpless one across from it. Red and yellow earth was sluicing away from beneath it. It began to lean, the water sucking it down. Then all at once, dynamite blasted thunderously. After that there was the sound of water breaking free, cutting around the dam and seeking the ditch, and Grif watched it leap boisterously away.

He ran past the downed man to the bulkhead, got the big iron wheel in his hands, and began to turn it. And just as he saw Broderick's stream begin to fail, he saw his own start up. Out of the boulders poured Matson and the others to man the Long Tom. Grif had to watch the fun from there, with an eye out for anyone attempting to open the valve again.

But somehow they seemed too busy to trace the trouble to its source. A gravel bank came sliding down, taking half a dozen men with it. Stones rolled and a distributor toppled, cut loose from its foundation. The tiller of the Long Tom was wrenched from Broderick's hands. He scrambled back to the rocks, and guns began to flare.

But even that was only a gesture. Those roaring tons of water were creating too much hell to allow anyone to take aim. But the men across the cañon had the leisure to hunt targets. Porter himself stumbled from the brush and slid into the stream. Broderick turned to climb the hill; the hard fist of the water found him, knocked him down, dragged him into the river of slickens he himself had created. In that muck there was no swimming. Watching for Broderick to come up, Grif remembered the day on Deer Creek. Broderick's body did not rise. The river had taken him to itself.

With all opposition beaten down, Matson turned the stream against the concentrate mill. Not until the barn-like structure collapsed did the hoarse shout of the monitor cease. . . .

They talked about the fight in the saloons of Indian Valley that night. They got drunk on it. They made plans on it. In the office of the Mountain Stage Company some plans were being made, too. Kip Matson didn't see where they could lose anything by sort of merging the two lines. "There's more traffic than we can handle, anyway," he declared. "Between the three of us we can corral all the business in the Sierras eventually. How about it?"

Grif looked at Katie. "It's all right with me. Any objections?"

Katie looked at Kip with her lips pressed together. "Just one. If we do it, I want to stipulate that nobody in the firm. . . ."

Kip said: "I know. . . ." He dug a half-eaten plug of chewing tobacco out of his pocket and handed it to Grif. "If you run across anybody that chaws, Grif, give him this. I've quit."

"Hard on the teeth?" Grif grinned.

Kip said: "Yeah. Hard on the heart, too, sometimes!"